THE BILLIONAIRE
OF CORAL BAY

THE BILLIONAIRE
OF CORAL BAY

BY

NIKKI LOGAN

First published in Great Britain 2017
By Mills & Boon, an imprint of HarperCollins*Publishers*
1 London Bridge Street, London, SE1 9GF

Large Print edition 2017

© 2017 Nikki Logan

ISBN: 978-0-263-07107-8

Our policy is to use papers that are natural, renewable
and recyclable products and made from wood grown
in sustainable forests. The logging and manufacturing
processes conform to the legal environmental regulations
of the country of origin.

Printed and bound in Great Britain
by CPI Antony Rowe, Chippenham, Wiltshire

For Pete
Who came when I needed him most.

CHAPTER ONE

THE LUXURY CATAMARAN had first appeared two days ago, bobbing in the sea off Nancy's Point.

Lurking.

Except Mila Nakano couldn't, in all fairness, call it lurking since it stood out like a flashing white beacon against the otherwise empty blue expanse of ocean. Whatever its crew were doing out there, they weren't trying to be secretive about it, which probably meant they had permission to be moored on the outer fringes of the reef. And a vessel with all the appropriate authorisation was no business of a Wildlife Officer with somewhere else to be.

Vessels came and went daily on the edge of the Marine Park off Coral Bay—mostly research boats, often charters and occasionally private yachts there to enjoy the World Heritage reefs. This one had 'private' written all over it. If she had the kind of money that bought luxury catamarans she'd probably spend it visiting places of wonder too.

Mila peeled her wetsuit down to its waist and let her eyes flutter shut as the coastal air against her sweat-damp skin tinkled like tiny, bouncing ball bearings. Most days, she liked to snorkel in just a bikini to revel in the symphony of water against her bare flesh. Some days, though, she just needed to get things done and a wetsuit was as good as noise-cancelling headphones to someone with synaesthesia—or 'superpower' as her brothers had always referred to her cross-sensed condition—because she couldn't *hear* the physical sensation of swimming over the reef when it was muted by thick neoprene. Not that her condition was conveniently limited to just the single jumbled sensation; no, that would be too pedestrian for Mila Nakano. She *felt* colours. She *tasted* emotion. And she attributed random personality traits to things. It might make no sense to anyone else but it made total sense to her.

Of course it did; she'd been born that way.

But today she could do without the distraction. Her tour-for-one was due any minute and she still needed to cross the rest of the bay and clamber up to Nancy's Point to meet him, because she'd drifted further than she meant while snorkelling the reef. A tour-for-one was the perfect number. *One* made it possible for her to do her job without ending up with a thumping headache—complete with harmonic foghorns. With larger groups, she couldn't control how shouty their body spray was, what mood the colours they wore would leave her in, or how exhausting they were just to be around. They would have a fantastic time out on the reef, but the cost to her was sometimes too great. It could take her three days to rebalance after a big group.

But one… That was doable.

Her *one* was a Mr Richard Grundy. Up from Perth, the solitary, sprawling metropolis on Australia's west coast, tucked away in the bottom corner of the state, two days' drive—or a two-hour jet flight—from here. From *anything*, some visitors thought because they couldn't see what was right in front of them. The vast expanses of outback scrub you had to pass through to get here.

The nothing that was always full of something.

Grundy was a businessman, probably, since

ones tended to arrive in suits with grand plans for the reef and what they could make it into. Anything from clusters of glamping facilities to elite floating casinos. Luxury theme parks. They never got off the ground, of course; between the public protests, the strict land use conditions and the flat-out *no* that the local leaseholder gave on development access through their property, her tour-for-one usually ended up being a tour-*of-* one. She never saw them, their business suit or their fancy development ideas again.

Which was fine; she was happy to play her part in keeping everything around here exactly as it was.

Mila shed the rest of her wetsuit unselfconsciously, stretched to the heavens for a moment as the ball bearings tinkled around her bikini-clad skin and slipped into the khaki shorts and shirt that identified her as official staff of the World Heritage Area. The backpack sitting on the sand bulged first with the folded wetsuit and then with bundled snorkelling gear, and she pulled her dripping hair back into a ponytail. She dropped the backpack into her work-supplied four-wheel drive then jogged past it and up towards the point over-looking the long, brilliant bay.

She didn't rush. *Ones* were almost always late; they underestimated the time it took to drive up from the city or down from the nearest airport, or they let some smartphone app decide how long it would take them when a bit of software could have no idea how much further a kilometre was in Western Australia's north. Besides, she'd parked on the only road into the meeting point and so her *one* would have had to drive past her to get to Nancy's Point. So far, hers was the only vehicle as far as the eye could see.

If you didn't count the bobbing catamaran beyond the reef.

Strong legs pushed her up over the lip of the massive limestone spur named after Nancy Dawson—the matriarch of the family that had grazed livestock on these lands for generations. Coral Bay's first family.

'Long way to come for a strip-show,' a deep voice rumbled as she straightened.

Mila stumbled to a halt, her stomach sinking on a defensive whiff of old shoe that was more back-of-her-throat *taste* than nose-scrunching *smell*.

The man standing there was younger than his name suggested and he wasn't in a suit, like most *ones*, but he wore cargo pants and a faded red T-shirt as if they were one. Something about the way he moved towards her... He still screamed 'corporate' even without a tie.

Richard Grundy.

She spun around, hunting for the vehicle that she'd inexplicably missed. Nothing. It only confounded her more. The muted red of his T-shirt was pumping off all kinds of favourite drunk uncle kind of associations, but she fought the instinctive softening that brought. Nothing about his sarcastic greeting deserved congeniality. Besides, this man was anything but uncle-esque. His dark blond hair was windblown but well-cut and his eyes, as he slid his impenetrable sunglasses up onto his head to reveal them, were a rich blue. Rather like the lagoon behind him, in fact.

That got him a reluctant bonus point.

'You were early,' she puffed.

'I was on time,' he said again, apparently amused at her discomfort. 'And I was dropped off. Just in time for the show.'

She retracted that bonus point. This was *her* bay, not his. If she wanted to swim in it before her shift started, what business was it of his?

'I could have greeted you in my wetsuit,' she muttered, 'but I figured my uniform would be more appropriate.'

'You're the guide, I assume?' he said, approaching with an out-thrust hand.

'I'm *a* guide,' she said, still bristling, then extended hers on a deep breath. Taking someone's hand was never straightforward; she never knew quite what she'd get out of it. 'Mila Nakano. Parks Department.'

'Richard Grundy,' he replied, marching straight into her grasp with no further greeting. Or interest. 'What's the plan for today?'

The muscles around her belly button twittered at his warm grip on her water-cool fingers and her ears filled with the gentle brush of a harp. That was new; she usually got anything from a solo trumpet to a whole brass section when she touched people, especially strangers.

A harp thrum was incongruously pleasant.

'Today?' she parroted, her synapses temporarily disconnected.

'Our tour.' His lagoon-coloured eyes narrowed in on hers. '*Are* you my guide?'

She quickly recovered. 'Yes, I am. But no one gave me any information on the purpose of your visit—' except to impress upon her his VIP status '—so we'll be playing it a bit by ear today. It would help me to know what you're here for,' she went on. 'Or what things interest you.'

'It all interests me,' he said, glancing away. 'I'd like to get a better appreciation for the...ecological value of the area.'

Uh-huh. Didn't they all...? Then they went back to the city to work on ways to exploit it.

'Is your interest commercial?'

The twin lagoons narrowed. 'Why so much interest in my interest?'

His censure made her flush. 'I'm just wondering what filter to put on the tour. Are you a journalist? A scientist? You don't seem like a tourist. So that only leaves Corporate.'

He glanced out at the horizon again, taking some of the intensity from their conversation. 'Let's just say I have a keen interest in the land. And the fringing reef.'

That wasn't much to go on. But those ramrod shoulders told her it was all she was going to get.

'Well, then, I guess we should start at the southernmost tip of the Marine Park,' she said, 'and work our way north. Can you swim?'

One of his eyebrows lifted. Just the one, as if her question wasn't worth the effort of a second. 'Captain of the swim team.'

Of course he had been.

Ordinarily she would have pushed her sunglasses up onto her head too, to meet a client's gaze, to start the arduous climb from *stranger* to *acquaintance*. But there was a sardonic heat coming off Richard Grundy's otherwise cool eyes and it shimmered such a curious tone—like five sounds all at once, harmonising with each other, being five different things at once. It wiggled in under her synaesthesia and tingled there, but she wasn't about to expose herself too fully to his music until she had a better handle on the man. And so her own sunglasses stayed put.

'If you want to hear the reef you'll need to get out onto it.'

'Hear it?' The eyebrow lift was back. 'Is it particularly noisy?'

She smiled. She'd yet to meet anyone else who could perceive the coral's voice but she had to assume that however normal people experienced it, it was as rich and beautiful as the way she did.

'You'll understand when you get there. Your vehicle or mine?'

But he didn't laugh—he didn't even smile—and her flimsy joke fell as flat as she inexplicably felt robbed of the opportunity to see his lips crack the straight line they'd maintained since she got up here.

'Yours, I think,' he said.

'Let's go, then.' She fell into professional mode, making up for a lot of lost time. 'I'll tell you about Nancy's Point as we walk. It's named for Nancy Dawson...'

Rich was pretty sure he knew all there was to know about Nancy Dawson—after all, stories of his great-grandmother had been part of his upbringing. But the tales as they were told to him didn't focus on Nancy's great love for the land and visionary sustainability measures, as the guide's did, they were designed to showcase her endurance and fortitude against adversity.

Those were the values his father had wanted to foster in his son and heir. The land—except for the profit it might make for WestCorp—was secondary. Barely even that.

But there was no way to head off the lithe young woman's spiel without confessing who his family was. And he wasn't about to discuss his private business with a stranger on two minutes' acquaintance.

'For one hundred and fifty years the Dawsons have been the leaseholders of all the land as far as you can see to the horizon,' she said, turning to put the ocean behind her and looking east. 'You could drive two hours inland and still be on Wardoo Station.'

'Big,' he grunted. Because anyone else would say that. Truth was, he knew exactly how big Wardoo was—to the square kilometre—and he knew how much each of those ten thousand square kilometres yielded. And how much each one cost to operate.

That was kind of his thing.

Rich cast his eyes out to the reef break. Mila apparently knew enough history to speak about his family, but not enough to recognise his surname for what it was. Great-Grandma Dawson had married Wardoo's leading hand, Jack Grundy, but kept the family name since it was such an established and respected name in the region. The world might have known Jack and Nancy's offspring as Dawsons, but the law knew them as Grundys.

'Nancy's descendants still run it today. Well, their minions do...'

That drew his gaze back. 'Minions?'

'The family is based in the city now. We don't see them.'

Wow. There was a whole world of judgement in that simple sentence.

'Running a business remotely is pretty standard procedure these days,' he pointed out.

In his world everything was run at a distance. In a state this big it was both an operational necessity and a survival imperative. If you got attached to any business—or any of the people in it—you couldn't do what he sometimes had to do. Restructure them. Sell them. Close them.

She surveyed all around them and murmured, 'If this was my land I would never ever leave it.'

It was tempting to take offence at her casual

judgement of his family—was this how she spoke of the Dawsons to any passing stranger?—but he'd managed too many teams and too many board meetings with voices far more objectionable than hers to let himself be that reactive. Besides, given that his 'family' consisted of exactly one—if you didn't count a bunch of headstones and some distant cousins in Europe—he really had little cause for complaint.

'You were born here?' he asked instead.

'And raised.'

'How long have your family lived in the area?'

'All my life—'

That had to be…what…? All of two decades?

'And thirty thousand years before that.'

He adjusted his assessment of her killer tan. That bronze-brown hue wasn't only about working outdoors. 'You're Bayungu?'

She shot him a look and he realised that he risked outing himself with his too familiar knowledge of Coral Bay's first people. That could reasonably lead to questions about why he'd taken the time to educate himself about the traditional uses of this area. Same reason he was here finding out about the environmental aspects of the region.

He wanted to know exactly what he was up against. Where the speed humps were going to arise.

'My mother's family,' she corrected softly.

Either she didn't understand how genetics worked or Mila didn't identify as indigenous despite her roots.

'But not only Bayungu? Nakano, I think you said?'

'My grandfather was Japanese. On Dad's side.'

He remembered reading that in the feasibility study on this whole coast: how it was a cultural melting pot thanks to the exploding pearling trade.

'That explains the bone structure,' he said, tracing his gaze across her face.

She flushed and seemed to say the first thing that came to her. 'His wife's family was from Dublin, just to complicate things.'

Curious that she saw her diversity as a *complication*. In business, it was a strength. Pretty much the first thing he'd done following his father's death was broaden WestCorp's portfolio base so that their eggs were spread across more baskets. Thirty-eight baskets, to be specific.

'What did Irish Grandma give you?' Rich glanced at her dark locks. 'Not red hair...'

'One of my brothers got that,' she acknowledged, stopping to consider him before sliding her sunglasses up onto her head. 'But I got Nan's eyes.'

Whoa...

A decade ago, he'd abseiled face-first down a cliff for sport—fast. The suck of his unprepared guts had been the same that day as the moment Mila's thick dark lashes lifted just now to reveal what they hid. Classic Celtic green. Not notable on their own, perhaps, but bloody amazing against the richness of her unblemished brown skin. Her respective grandparents had certainly left her a magnetising genetic legacy.

He used the last of his air replying. 'You're a walking billboard for cultural diversity.'

She glanced away, her mocha skin darkening, and he could breathe again. But it wasn't some coy affectation on her part. She looked genuinely distressed—though she was skilled at hiding it.

Fortunately, he was more skilled at reading people.

'The riches of the land and sea up here have always drawn people from around the world,' she murmured. 'I'm the end result.'

They reached her modest four-wheel drive, emblazoned with government logos, halfway down the beach she'd first emerged from, all golden and glittery.

'Is that why you stay?' he asked. 'Because of the riches?'

She looked genuinely horrified at the thought as she unlocked the vehicle and swung her long sandy legs in. 'Not in the sense you mean. My work is here. My family is here. My heart is here.'

And clearly she wore that heart on the sleeve of her Parks Department uniform.

Rich climbed in after her and gave a little inward sigh. Sailing north on the *Portus* had been seven kinds of awesome. All the space and quiet and air he needed wrapped up in black leather and oiled deck timber. He'd even unwound a little. But there was something about driving... Four wheels firm on asphalt. Owning the road.

Literally, in this case.

At least for the next few months. Longer, if he got his way.

'Is that why you're here?' she asked him, though it looked as if she had to summon up a fair bit of courage to do it. 'Drawn by the riches?'

If he was going to spend the day with her he wasn't going to be able to avoid the question for long. Might as well get in front of it.

'I'm here to find out everything I can about the area. I have…business interests up here. I'd like to go in fully informed.'

Her penetrating gaze left him and turned back to the road, leaving only thinned lips in its wake.

He'd disappointed her.

'The others wanted to know a bit about the history of Coral Bay.' She almost sighed. 'Do you?'

It was hard not to smile at her not so subtle angling. He was probably supposed to say *What others?* and she was going to tell him how many people had tried and failed to get developments up in this region. Maybe he was even supposed to be deterred by that.

Despite Mila's amateurish subterfuge, he played along. A few friendly overtures wouldn't go amiss. Even if she didn't look all that disposed to overtures of any kind—friendly or otherwise. Her job meant she kind of had to.

He settled into the well-worn fabric. 'Sure. Take me right back.'

She couldn't possibly maintain her coolness once she got stuck into her favourite topic. As long as Mila was talking, he had every excuse to just watch her lips move and her eyes flash with engagement. If nothing else, he could enjoy that.

She started with the ancient history of the land that they drove through, how this flat coast had been seafloor in the humid time before mammals. Then, a hundred million years later when the oceans were all locked up in a mini ice age and sea levels had retreated lower than they'd ever been, how her mother's ancestors had walked the shores on the edge of the massive continental drop-off that was now five kilometres out to sea. Many of the fantastical creatures of the Saltwater People's creation stories might well have been perfectly literal, hauled out of the deep sea trenches even with primitive tools.

The whole time she talked, Rich watched, entranced. Hiring Mila to be an ambassador for this place was an inspired move on someone's part.

She was passionate and vivid. Totally engaged in what was obviously her favourite topic. She sold it in a way history books couldn't possibly.

But the closer she brought him to contemporary times, the more quirks he noticed in her storytelling. At first, he thought it was just the magical language of the tribal stories—evocative, memorable…almost poetic—but then he realised some of the references were too modern to be part of traditional tales.

'Did you just call the inner reef "smug"?' he interrupted.

She glanced at him, mid-sentence. Swallowing. 'Did I?'

'That's what I heard.'

Her knuckles whitened on the steering wheel. 'Are you sure I didn't say warm? That's what I meant. Because it's shallower inside the reef. The sand refracts sunlight and leads to—' she paused for half a heartbeat '—warmer conditions that the coral really thrives in.'

Her gaze darted around for a moment before she continued and he got the distinct feeling he'd just been lied to.

Again, though, amateurish.

This woman could tell one hell of a tale but she would be a sitting duck in one of his boardrooms.

'Ten thousand years from now,' she was continuing, and he forced himself to attend, 'those reef areas out there will emerge from the water and form atolls and, eventually, the certainty of earth.'

He frowned at her augmented storytelling. It didn't diminish her words particularly but the longer it went on the more overshadowing it became until he stopped listening to *what* she was saying and found himself only listening to *how* she said it.

'There are vast gorges at the top of the cape that tourists assume are made purely of cynical rock, but they're not. They were once reef too, tens of millions of years ago, until they got thrust up above the land by tectonic plate action. The enduring limestone is full of marine fossils.'

Cynical rock. *Certain* earth. *Enduring* limestone. The land seemed alive for Mila Nakano— almost a person, with its own traits—but it didn't irritate him because it wasn't an affectation and it didn't diminish the quality of her information at all. When she called the reef *smug* he got the sense that she believed it and, because she believed it, it just sounded…possible. If he got to lie about in warm water all day being nibbled free of parasites by a harem of stunning fish he'd be pretty smug too.

'I'd be interested to see those gorges,' he said, more to spur her on to continue her hyper-descriptive storytelling than anything else. Besides, something like that was just another string in his bow when it came to creating a solid business case for his resort.

She glanced at him. 'No time. We would have had to set off much earlier. The four-wheel drive access has been under three metres of curi—'

She caught herself and he couldn't help wondering what she'd been about to say.

'Of sea water for weeks. We'd have to go up the eastern side of the cape and come in from the north. It's a long detour.'

His disappointment was entirely disproportionate to her refusal—sixty seconds ago he'd had zero interest in fossils or gorges—but he found himself eager to make it happen.

'What if we had a boat?'

'Well, that would be faster, obviously.' She set

her eyes back on the road ahead and then, at this silent expectation, returned them to him. '*Do* you have one?'

He'd never been prouder to have the *Portus* lingering offshore. But he wasn't ready to reveal her just yet. 'I might be able to get access...'

Her green gaze narrowed just slightly. 'Then this afternoon,' she said. 'Right now we have other obligations.'

'We do?'

She hit the indicator even though there were no other road-users for miles around, and turned off the asphalt onto a graded limestone track. Dozens of tyre-tracks marked its dusty white surface.

'About time you got wet, Mr Grundy.'

CHAPTER TWO

BELOW THE SLIGHTLY elevated parking clearing at Five Fingers Bay, the limestone reef stretched out like the splayed digits in the beach's name. They formed a kind of catwalk, pointing out in five directions to the outer reef beyond the lagoon. Mila led her *one* down to it and stood on what might have been the Fingers' exposed rocky wrist.

'I was expecting more *Finding Nemo*,' he said, circling to look all around him and sounding as disappointed as the sag of his shoulders, 'and less *Flintstones*. Where's all the sea life?'

'What you want is just out there, Mr Grundy.'

He followed her finger out beyond the stretch of turquoise lagoon to the place the water darkened off, marking the start of the back reef that kept most predators—and most boats—out, all the way up to those gorges that he wanted to visit.

'Call me Richard,' he volunteered. 'Rich.'

Uh, no. 'Rich' was a bit too like friends and—

given what he was up here for—even calling
them acquaintances was a stretch. Besides, she
wasn't convinced by his sudden attempt at gra-
ciousness.

'Richard...' Mila allowed, conscious that she
represented her department. She rummaged in
the rucksack she'd dragged from the back seat
of the SUV. 'I have a spare mask and snorkel for
you.'

He stared at them as if they were entirely for-
eign, but then reached out with a firm hand and
took them from her. She took care not to let her
fingers brush against his.

It was always awkward, taking your clothes off
in front of a stranger; it was particularly uncomfortable in front of a young, handsome stranger,
but Mila turned partly away, shrugged out of
her work shorts and shirt and stood in her bikini, fiddling with the adjustment straps on her
mask while Richard shed his designer T-shirt
and cargo pants.

She kept her eyes carefully averted, not out
of any prudishness but because she always approached new experiences with a moment's care.
She could never tell how something new was

going to impact on her and, while she'd hung out with enough divers and surfers to give her some kind of certainty about what senses a half-naked person would trigger—apples for some random guy peeling off his wetsuit, watermelon for a woman pulling hers on—this was a *new* half-naked man. And a client.

She watched his benign shadow on the sand until she was sure he'd removed everything he was going to.

Only then did she turn around.

Instantly, she was back at the only carnival she'd ever visited, tucking into her first—and last—candyfloss. The light, sticky cloud dissolving into pure sugar on her tongue. The smell of it, the taste of it. That sweet, sweet rush. She craved it instantly. It was so much more intense—and so much more humiliating—than a plain old apples association. But apparently that was what her synaesthesia had decided to associate with a half-naked Richard Grundy.

The harmless innocence of that scent was totally incompatible with a man she feared was here to exploit the reef. But that was how it went;

her associations rarely had any logical connection with their trigger.

Richard had come prepared with navy board shorts beneath his expensive but casual clothes. They were laced low and loose on his hips yet still managed to fit snugly all the way down his muscular thighs.

And they weren't even wet yet.

Mila filled her lungs slowly and mastered her gaze. He might not be able to read her dazed thoughts but he might well be able to read her face and so she turned back to her rummaging. Had her snorkelling mask always been this fiddly to adjust?

'I only have one set of fins, sorry,' she said in a rush. 'Five Fingers is good for drift snorkelling, though, so you can let the water do the work.'

She set off up the beach a way so that they could let the current carry them back near to their piled up things by the end of the swim. Her slog through sun-soaked sand was accompanied by the high-pitched single note that came with a warmth so everyday that she barely noticed it anymore. When they reached the old reef, she turned seaward and walked into the water without a backward glance—she didn't need the sugary distraction and she felt certain Richard would follow her in without invitation. They were snorkelling on his dollar, after all.

'So coral's not a plant?' Richard asked once they were waist-deep in the electric-blue water of the lagoon.

She paused and risked another look at him. Prepared this time. 'It's an animal. Thousands of tiny animals, actually, living together in the form of elk horns, branches, plates, cabbages—'

He interrupted her shopping list ramble with the understated impatience of someone whose time really was money. Only the cool water prevented her from blushing. Did she always babble this much with clients? Or did it only feel like babbling in Richard Grundy's presence?

'So how does a little squishy thing end up becoming rock-hard reef?' he asked.

Good. Yes. Focusing on the science kept the candyfloss at bay. Although as soon as he'd said 'rock-hard' she'd become disturbingly fixated on the remembered angles of his chest and had to severely discipline her unruly gaze not to follow suit.

'The calcium carbonate in their skeletons. In life, it provides resilience against the sea currents, and in death—'

She braced on her left leg as she slipped her right into her mono-fin. Then she straightened and tucked her left foot in with it and balanced there on the soft white seafloor. The gentle waves rocked her a little in her rooted spot, just like one of the corals she was describing.

'In death they pile up to form limestone reef,' he guessed.

'Millions upon millions of them forming reef first, then limestone that weathers into sand, and finally scrubland grows on top of it. We owe a lot to coral, really.'

Mila took a breath and turned to face him, steadfastly ignoring the smell of carnival. 'Ready to meet the reef?'

He glanced out towards the reef break and swallowed hard. It was the first time she'd seen him anything other than supremely confident, verging on arrogant.

'How far out are we going?'

'Not very. That's the beauty of Coral Bay; the inside reef is right there, the moment you step offshore. The lagoon is narrow but long. We'll be travelling parallel to the beach, mostly.'

His body lost some of its rigidity and he took a moment to fit his mask and snorkel before stepping off the sandy ridge after her.

It took no time to get out where the seafloor dropped away enough that they could glide in the cool water two metres above the reef. The moment Mila submerged, the synaesthetic symphony began. It was a mix of the high notes caused by the water rushing over her bare skin and the vast array of sounds and sensations caused by looking down at the natural metropolis below in all its diversity. Far from the flat, gently sloping, sandy sea bottom that people imagined, coral reef towered in places, dropped away in others, just like any urban centre. There were valleys and ridges and little caves from where brightly coloured fish surveyed their personal square metre of territory. Long orange antenna poked out from under a shelf and acted as the early warning system of a perky, pincers-at-the-ready crayfish. Anemones danced smooth and slow on the current, their base firmly tethered to the reef, stinging anything that came close but giving the little fish happily living inside it a free pass in return for its nibbly housekeeping.

Swimming over the top of it all, peering down through the glassy water, it felt like cruising above an alien metropolis in some kind of silent-running airship—just the sound of her own breathing inside the snorkel, and her myriad synaesthetic associations in her mind's ear. The occasional colourful little fellow came up to have a closer look at them but mostly the fish just went about their business, adhering to the strict social rules of reef communities, focusing on their eternal search for food, shelter or a mate.

Life was pretty straightforward under the surface.

And it was insanely abundant.

She glanced at Richard, who didn't seem to know where to look first. His mask darted from left to right, taking in the coral city ahead of them, looking below them at some particular point. He'd tucked his hands into balls by his hips and she wondered if that was to stop him reaching out and touching the strictly forbidden living fossil.

She took a breath and flipped gently in the water, barely flexing her mono-fin to effect the move, swimming backwards ahead of him so that she could see if he was doing okay. His mask came up square onto hers and, even in the electric-blue underworld, his eyes still managed to stand out as they locked on hers.

And he smiled.

The candyfloss returned with a vengeance. It was almost overpowering in the cloistered underwater confines of her mask. Part of her brain knew it wasn't real but as far as the other part was concerned she was sucking her air directly from some carnival tent. That was the first smile she'd seen from Richard and it was a doozy, even working around a mouthful of snorkel. It transformed his already handsome face into something really breath-stealing and, right now, she needed all the air she could get!

She signalled upwards, flicked her fin and was back above the glassy surface within a couple of heartbeats.

'I've spent so much time on the water and I had no idea there was so much going on below!' he said the moment his mouth was free of rub-

bery snorkel. 'I mean you know but you don't…
know. You know?'

This level of inarticulateness wasn't uncommon for someone seeing the busy reef for the first time—their minds were almost always blown—but it made her feel just a little bit better about how much of a babbler she'd been with him.

His finless legs had to work much harder than hers to keep him perpendicular to the water and his breath started to grow choppy. 'It's so…structured. Almost city-like.'

Mila smiled. It was so much easier to relate to someone over the reef.

'Coral polyps organise into a stag horn just like a thousand humans organise into a high-rise building. It's a futuristic city…with hovercraft. Ready for more?'

His answer was to bite back down onto his snorkel's mouthpiece and tip himself forward, back under the surface.

They drifted on for another half-hour and she let Richard take the lead, going where interest took him. He got more skilled at the suspension of breath needed to deep snorkel, letting him get closer to the detail of the reef, and the two of

them were like mini whales every time they surfaced, except they blew water instead of air from
their clumsy plastic blowholes.

There was something intimate in the way they
managed to expel the water at the same time on
surfacing—relaxed, not urgent—then take another breath and go back for more. Over and over
again. It was vaguely like…

Kissing.

Mila's powerful kick pushed her back up to the
surface. That was not a thought she was about
to entertain. He was a *one*, for a start, and he
was here to exploit the very reef he was cur-
rently going crazy over. Though if she did her
job then maybe he'd change his mind about that
after today.

'Seen enough?' she asked when he caught up
with her.

His mask couldn't hide the disappointment behind it. 'Is it time to go in?'

'I just want to show you the drop-off, then we'll
head back to the beach.'

Just was probably an understatement, and
they'd have to swim out of the shallow waters
towards the place the continental shelf took its

first plunge, but for Richard to understand the reef and how it connected to the oceanic ecosystem he needed to see it for himself.

Seeing was believing.

Unless you were her, in which case, seeing came with a whole bunch of other sensations that no one else experienced. Or necessarily believed.

She'd lost enough friends in the past to recognise that.

Mila slid the mouthpiece back into her snorkel and tooted out of the top.

'Let's go.'

Richard prided himself on being a man of composure. In the boardroom, in the bedroom, in front of a media pack. In fact, it was something he was known for—courage under fire—and it came from always knowing your strengths, and your opponents'. From always doing your homework. From controlling all the variables before they even had time to vary.

This had to be the least composed he'd been in a long, long time.

Mila had swum alongside him, her vigilant eyes sweeping around them so that he could just enjoy the wonders of the reef, monitoring their position to make sure they didn't get caught up in the current. He'd felt the change in the water as the outer reef had started to rise up to meet them, almost shore-like. But it wasn't land; it was the break line one kilometre out from the actual shore where the reef grew most abundant and closest to the surface of anywhere they'd swum yet. So close, the waves from the deeper water on the other side crashed against it relentlessly and things got a little choppier than their earlier efforts. Mila had led him to a channel that allowed them to propel themselves down between the high-rise coral—just like any of the reef's permanent residents—and get some relief from the surging waves as they'd swum out towards a deeper, darker, more distant kind of blue. The water temperature had dropped and the corals started to change—less of the soft, flowy variety interspersed with dancing life and more of the slow-growing, rock-hard variety. Coral mean streets. The ones that could withstand the water pressure coming at them from the open ocean twenty-four-seven.

Rich lifted his eyes and tried to make something out in the deep blue visible beyond the coral valley he presently lurked in. He couldn't—just a graduated, ill-defined shift from blue to deep blue to dark blue looking out and down. No scale. No end point. Impossible to get a grip on how far this drop-off actually went.

It even had the word 'drop' in it.

His pulse kicked up a notch.

Mila swam on ahead, rising briefly to refill her lungs and sinking again to swim out through the opening of the coral valley straight into all that vast blue…nothing.

And that was where his courage flat ran out.

He'd played hard contact sports, he'd battled patronising boardroom jerks, he'd wrangled packs of media wolves hell-bent on getting a story, and he'd climbed steep rock faces for fun. None of those things were for the weak-willed. But could he bring himself to swim past the break and out into the place the reef—and the entire country—dropped off to open, bottomless ocean?

Nope.

He tried—not least because of Mila, back-swimming so easily out into the unknown, her dark hair floating all around her, mermaid tail

waving gently at him like a beckoning finger—
but even that was not enough to seduce him out
there. The vast blue was so impossible to position
himself in, he found himself constantly glancing
up to the bright surface where the sunlight was,
just to keep himself oriented. Or back at the reef
edge to have the certainty of it behind him.

Swimming out over the drop-off was as inconceivable to him as stepping off a mountain. His
body simply would not comply.

As if it had some information he didn't.

And Richard Grundy made it his priority always to have the information he needed.

'It's okay,' Mila sputtered gently, surfacing next
to him once they'd moved back to the side of the
reef protected from the churn of the crest. 'The
drop-off's not easy the first time.'

No. What wasn't easy was coming face to face
with a limitation you never knew you had, and
doing it in front of a slip of a thing who clearly
didn't suffer the same disability. Who looked as
if she'd been born beneath the surface.

'The current...' he hedged.

As if that had anything to do with it. He knew
Mila wouldn't have taken him somewhere un-

safe. Not that he knew her at all, and yet some-how…he did. She just didn't seem the type to be intentionally unkind. And her job relied on her getting her customers back to shore in one piece.

'Let's head in,' she said.

There was a thread of charity in her voice that he was not comfortable hearing. He didn't need anyone else's help recognising his deficiencies or to be patronised, no matter how well-meant. This would always be the first thing she thought of when she thought of him, no matter what else he achieved.

The guy that couldn't swim the drop-off.

It only took ten minutes to swim back in when he wasn't distracted by the teeming life beneath them. Thriving, living coral turned to rocky old reef, reef turned to sand and then his feet were finding the seafloor and pushing him upwards. He'd never felt such a weighty slave to gravity—it was as indisputable as the instinct that had stopped him swimming out into all that blue.

Survival.

Mila struggled a little to get her feet out of her single rubber fin and he stepped closer so she could use him as a brace. She glanced at him sideways for a moment with something that looked a lot like discomfort before politely resting her hand on his forearm and using him for balance while she prised first one and then the other foot free. As she did it she even held her breath.

Really? Had he diminished himself that much? She didn't even want to *touch* him?

'That was the start of the edge of Australia's continental shelf,' she said when she was back on two legs. 'The small drop-off slopes down to the much bigger one five kilometres out—'

Small?

'And then some of the most immense deep-sea trenches on the planet.'

'Are you trying to make me feel better?' he said tightly.

And had failing always been this excruciating?

Her pretty face twisted a little. 'No. But your body might have been responding instinctively to that unknown danger.'

'I deal with unknowns every day.'

Dealt with them and redressed them. WestCorp thrived on *knowns*.

'Do you, really?' she asked, tipping her glance

towards him, apparently intent on placating him with conversation. 'When was the last time you did something truly new to you?'

Part of the reason he dominated in business was because nothing fazed him. Like a good game of chess, there was a finite number of plays to address any challenge and once you'd perfected them the only contest was knowing which one to apply. The momentary flare of satisfaction as the challenge tumbled was about all he had, these days. The rest was business as usual.

And outside of business…

Well, how long had it been since there was anything outside of business?

'I went snorkelling today,' he said, pulling off his mask.

'That was your first time? You did well, then.'

She probably meant to be kind, but all her condescension did was remind him why he never did anything before learning everything there was to know about it. Controlling his environment.

Open ocean was not a controlled environment.

'How about you?' he deflected as the drag of the water dropped away and they stepped onto toasty warm sand. 'You don't get bored of the same view every day? The same reef?'

She turned back out to the turquoise lagoon and the deeper blue sea beyond it—that same blue that he loved from the comfort and safety of his boat.

'Nope.' She sighed. 'I like a lot of familiarity in my environment because of—' she caught herself, turned back and changed tack '—because I'm at my best when it's just me and the ocean.'

He snorted. 'What's the point of being your best when no one's around to see it?'

He didn't mean to be dismissive, but he saw her reaction in the flash behind her eyes.

'I'm around.' She shrugged, almost embarrassed. 'I'll know.'

'And you reserve the best of yourself *for* yourself?' he asked, knowing any hope of a congenial day with her was probably already sunk.

Her curious gaze suggested he was more alien to her than some of the creatures they'd just been studying. 'Why would I give it to someone else?'

She crossed to their piled-up belongings and began to shove her snorkelling equipment into the canvas bag.

Rich pressed the beach towel she'd supplied to his chest as he watched her go, and disguised the full-body shiver that followed. But he couldn't blame it on the chilly water alone—there was something else at play here, something more... disquieting.

He patted his face dry with the sun-warmed fabric to buy himself a moment to identify the uncomfortable sensation.

For all his success—for all his professional renown—Rich suddenly had the most unsettling suspicion that he might have missed something fundamental about life.

Why *would* anyone give the best of themselves to someone else?

CHAPTER THREE

MILA NEVER LIKED to see any creature suffer—
even one as cocky as Richard Grundy—but,
somehow, suffering brought him closer to her
level than he'd yet been. More likeable and relat-
able Clark Kent, less fortress of solitude Super-
man. He'd taken the drop-off experience hard,
and he'd been finding any feasible excuse not to
make eye contact with her ever since.

Most people got no phone reception out of town
but Richard somehow did and he'd busied himself with a few business calls, including arrang-
ing for the boat he knew of to meet them at Bill's
Bay marina. It was indisputably the quickest way
to get to the gorges he wanted to see. All they
had to do was putter out of the State and Federal-
protected marine park, then turn north in open,
deregulated waters and power up the coast at
full speed, before heading back into the marine
park again. They could be there in an hour in-

stead of the three it would take by road. And the three back again.

It looked as if Richard would use every moment of that hour to focus on business.

Still, his distraction gave her time to study him. His hair had only needed a few strategic arrangements to get it back to a perfectly barbered shape, whereas hers was a tangled, salt-crusted mess. Side on, she could see behind his expensive sunglasses and knew just how blue those eyes were. The glasses sat comfortably on high cheekbones, which was where the designer stubble also happened to begin. It ran down his defined jaw and met its mirror image at a slightly cleft chin. As nice as all of that was—and it was; just the thought of how that stubble might feel under her fingers was causing a flurry of kettledrums, of all things—clearly its primary role in life was to frame what had to be his best asset. A killer pair of lips. Not too thin, not too full, perfectly symmetrical. Not at their best right now while he was still so tense, but earlier, when they'd broken out that smile...

Ugh...murder.

The car filled with the scent of spun sugar again.

'Something you need?'

He spoke without turning his eyes off the road ahead or prising the phone from his ear, but the twist of the mouth she'd just been admiring told her he was talking to her.

She'd meant to be subtle, glancing sideways, studying him in her periphery, yet apparently those lips were more magnetic than she realised because she was turned almost fully towards him. She snapped her gaze forward.

'No. Just…um…'

Just obsessing on your body parts, Mr Grundy…

Just wondering how I could get you to smile again, sir…

'We're nearly at the boat launch,' she fabricated. 'Just wanted you to know.'

If he believed her, she couldn't tell. He simply nodded, returned to his call and then took his sweet time finishing it.

Mila forced her mind back on the job.

'This is the main road in and out of Coral Bay,' she said as soon as he disconnected his call, turning her four-wheel drive at a cluster of towering solar panels that powered streetlights at the only intersection in the district. 'It's base camp for everyone wanting access to the southern part of the World Heritage area.'

To her, Coral Bay was a sweet, green little oasis existing in the middle of almost nowhere. No other town for two hundred kilometres in any direction. Just boundless, rust-coloured outback on one side and a quarter of a planet of ocean on the other.

Next stop, Africa.

Richard's eyes narrowed as they entered town and he saw all the caravans, RVs, four-by-fours and tour buses parked all along the main street. 'It's thriving.'

His interest reminded her of a cartoon she'd seen once where a rumpled-suited businessman's eyes had spun and rolled and turned into dollar signs. It was as if he was counting the potential.

'It's whale shark season. Come back in forty-degree February and it will be a ghost town. Summer is brutal up here.'

If he wanted to build some ritzy development, he might as well know it wasn't going to be a year-round goldmine.

'I guess that's what air-conditioning is for,' he murmured.

'Until the power station goes down in a cyclone, then you're on your own.'

His lips twisted, just slightly. 'You're not really selling the virtues of the region, you know.'

No. This wasn't her job. This was personal. She forced herself back on a professional footing.

'Did you want to stop in town? For something to eat, maybe? Snorkelling always makes me hungry.'

Plus, Coral Bay had the best bakery in the district, regardless of the fact it also had the only bakery in the district.

'We'll have lunch on the *Portus*,' he said absently.

The *Portus*? Not one of the boats that frequented Coral Bay. She knew them all by sight. It hadn't occurred to her that he might have access to a vessel from outside the region. Especially given he'd only called to make arrangements half an hour ago.

'Okay—' she shrugged, resigning herself to a long wait '—straight to Bill's Bay, then.'

They parked up on arrival at the newly appointed mini-marina and wandered down to where three others launched boats for a midday run. Compared to the elaborate 'tinnies' of the locals, getting their hulls wet on the ramp, the white Zodiac idling at the end of the single pier immediately caught her attention.

'There's Damo.' Rich raised a hand and the Zodiac's skipper acknowledged it as they approached. 'You look disappointed, Mila.'

Her gaze flew to his, not least because it was the first time he'd called her by her name. It eased off his lips like a perfectly cooked salmon folding off a knife.

'I underestimated how long it was going to take us to get north,' she said, flustered. 'It's okay; I'll adjust the schedule.'

'Were you expecting something with a bit more grunt?'

'No.' *Yes.*

'I really didn't know what to expect,' she went on. 'A boat is a boat, right? As long as it floats.'

He almost smiled then, but it was too twisted to truly earn the name. She cursed the missed moment. A tall man in the white version of her own shorts and shirt stood as they approached the end of the pier. He acknowledged Richard with a courteous nod, then offered her his arm aboard.

'Miss?'

She declined his proffered hand—not just because she needed little help managing embarkation onto such a modest vessel, but also because she could do without the associated sounds that generally came with a stranger's skin against hers.

The skipper was too professional to react. Richard, on the other hand, frowned at her dismissal of a man clearly doing him a favour.

Mila sighed. Okay, so he thought her rude. It wouldn't be the first time someone had assumed the worst. And she wouldn't be seeing him again after today, so what did it really matter?

The skipper wasted no time firing up the surprisingly throaty Zodiac and reversing them out of the marina and in between the markers that led bigger boats safely through the reef-riddled sanctuary zone towards more open waters. They ambled along at five knots and only opened up a little once they hit the recreation zone, where boating was less regulated. It took just a few minutes to navigate the passage that put them in open water, but the skipper didn't throttle right up like she expected; instead he kept his speed down as they approached a much larger and infinitely more expensive catamaran idling just beyond the outer reef. The vessel she'd seen earlier, at Nancy's Point. Slowing as they passed such a massive vessel seemed a back-to-front kind of courtesy, given the giant cat would barely feel their wake if they passed it at full speed. It was only as their little Zodiac swung around to reverse up to the catamaran that she saw the letters emblazoned on the big cat's side.

Portus.

'Did you think we were going all the way north in the tender?' a soft voice came to her over the thrum of the slowly reversing motor.

'Is this yours?' she asked, gaping.

'If she's not, we're getting an awfully accommodating reception for a couple of trespassers.'

'So when you said you were "dropped off" at Nancy's Point...?'

'I didn't mean in a car.'

With those simple words, his capacity to get his mystery development proposal through where others had failed increased by half in Mila's mind. A man with the keys to a vessel like this in his pocket had to have at least a couple of politicians there too, right?

The tender's skipper expertly reversed them backwards, right up to the stern of the *Portus,* where a set of steps came down each of the cat's two hulls to the waterline. A dive platform at the bottom of each served as a disembarkation point and she could see where the tender would nest in snugly under its mother vessel when it wasn't in use. Stepping off the back of the tender and onto the *Portus* was as easy as entering her house. Where the upward steps delivered them— to an outdoor area that would comfortably seat twelve—the vessel was trimmed out with timber and black leather against the boat's white fibreglass. Not vinyl... Not hardy canvas like most of the boats she'd been on. This was *leather*— soft and smooth under her fingers as she placed a light hand on the top of one padded seat-back. The sensation was accompanied by a percussion of wind chimes, low and sonorous.

Who knew she found leather so soothing!

The colour scheme was conflicting, emotionally, even as it was perfect visually. The tranquillity of white, the sensuality of black. Brown usually made her feel sad, but this particularly rich, oiled tone struck her more specifically as… isolated.

But it was impossible not to also acknowledge the truth.

'This is so beautiful, Richard.'

To her left, timber stairs spiralled up and out of view to the deck above.

'It does the job,' he said modestly, then pulled open two glass doors into the vessel's gorgeous interior, revealing an expansive dining area and a galley twice as big as her own kitchen.

She just stared at him until he noticed her silence.

'What?'

'Surely, even in your world this vessel is something special,' she said, standing firm on the threshold, as though she needed to get this resolved before entering. False humility was worse than an absence of it, and she had a blazing desire to have the truth from this man just once.

On principle.

'What do you know about my world?' he cast

back easily over his shoulder, seemingly uncaring whether she followed him or not.

She clung to *not* and hugged the doorway.

'You wouldn't have bought the boat if you didn't think it was special.'

He turned to face her. 'It wouldn't be seemly to boast about my own boat, Mila.'

'It would be honest.' And really, what was this whole vessel but big, mobile bragging rights? 'Or is it just saying the words aloud that bothers you?'

He turned to face her, but she barrelled on without really knowing why it affected her so much. Maybe it had something to do with growing up on two small rural incomes. Or maybe it had something to do with starting to think they might be closer to equals, only to be faced with the leather and timber evidence very much to the contrary.

'I'll say it for you,' she said from the doorway. 'The *Portus* is amazing. You must be incredibly relaxed when you're out on her.' She glanced at the massive dining table. 'And you must have some very happy friends.'

'I don't really bring friends out,' he murmured, regarding her across the space between them.

'Colleagues, then. Clients.'

He leaned back on the kitchen island and crossed his ankles. 'Nope. I like silence when I'm out on the water.'

She snorted. 'Good luck with that.' He just stared at her. 'I mean it's never truly silent, is it?'

He frowned at her. 'Isn't it?'

No. Not in her experience.

She glanced around as the *Portus*' massive engines thrummed into life and they began to move, killing any hope of silence for the time being. Although they weren't nearly as loud as she'd expected. How much did a boat have to cost to get muted engines like that?

Richard didn't invite her in again. Or insist. Or cajole. Instead, he leaned there, patience personified until she felt that her refusal to step inside was more than just ridiculous.

It was as unfriendly as people had always thought her to be.

But entering while he waited felt like too much of a concession in this mini battle of wills. She didn't want to see the flare of triumph in his eyes. Her own shifted to the double fridge at the heart of the galley.

'I guess lunch won't be cheese sandwiches out of an Esky, then?'

The moment his regard left her to follow her glance, she stepped inside, crossing more than just a threshold. She stepped wholly into Richard's fancy world.

He pulled the fridge doors wide. 'It's a platter. Crayfish. Tallegio. Salt and pepper squid. Salad Niçoise. Sourdough bread.'

She laughed. 'I guess I was wrong, then. Cheese sandwich it is.' Just fancier.

He turned his curiosity to her. 'You don't eat seafood?'

'I can eat prawns if I have to. And molluscs. They don't have a strong personality.'

That frown just seemed to be permanently fixed on his face. 'But cray and squid do?'

Her heart warmed just thinking about them and it helped to loosen her bones just a little. 'Very much so. Particularly crayfish. They're quite… optimistic.'

He stared—for several bemused moments— clearly deciding between *quirky* and *nuts*. Both of which she'd had before with a lot less subtlety than he was demonstrating.

'Is it going to bother you if I eat them?'

'No. Something tells me I won't be going hungry.' She smiled and it was easier than she expected. 'I have no strong feelings about cheese, either way.'

'Unlucky for the Tallegio then,' he murmured.

He pulled open a cabinet and revealed it as a small climate-controlled wine cellar. Room temperature on the left, frosty on the right. 'Red or white?' he asked.

'Neither,' she said regretfully. Just looking at the beading on the whites made her long for a dose of ocean spray. 'I'm on the clock.'

'Not right now you're not,' he pointed out. 'For the next ninety minutes, we're both in the capable hands of Captain Max Farrow, whose jurisdiction, under international maritime law, overrules your own.'

He lifted out one of the dewy bottles and waved it gently in her direction.

It was tempting to play at all this luxury just for a little while. To take a glass and curl up on one of those leather sofas, enjoy the associated wind chimes and act as if they weren't basically complete strangers. To talk like normal people. To pretend. At all of it.

'One glass, then,' she said. 'Thank you.'

He poured and handed her a glass of white. The silent moments afterwards sang with discomfort.

'Come on, I'll give you a tour,' he eventually offered.

He smiled but it didn't ring true and it certainly didn't set off the five-note harmony or the scent of candyfloss that the flash of perfect teeth previously had. He couldn't be as nervous as she was, surely. Was he also conscious of how make-believe this all was?

Even if, for him, it wasn't.

She stood. 'Thank you, Richard.'

'Rich,' he insisted. 'Please. Only my colleagues call me Richard.'

They were a good deal less than colleagues, but it would be impossible now to call him anything else without causing offence. *More* offence.

'Please, Mila. I think you'll like the *Portus*.' Then, when she still didn't move, he added, 'As much as I do.'

That one admission… That one small truth

wiggled right in under her ribs. Disarming her completely.

'I would love to see more, Rich, thank you.'

The name felt awkward on her lips and yet somehow right at the same time. Clunky but... okay, as if it could wear in comfortably with use.

The tour didn't take long, not because there wasn't a lot to look at in every sumptuous space but because, despite its size, the *Portus* was, as it happened, mostly boat. As Rich showed her around she noted a jet ski securely stashed at the back, a sea kayak, water skis—everything a man could need to enjoy some time *on* the water. But she saw nothing to indicate that he enjoyed time *in* it.

'No diving gear?' she commented. 'On a boat with not one but two dive decks?'

His pause was momentary. 'Plenty to keep me busy above the surface,' he said.

Something about that niggled in this new environment of truce between them. That little glimpse of vulnerability coming so close on the heels of some humble truth. But she didn't need super-senses to know not to push it. She carried on the tour in comparative silence.

The *Portus* primarily comprised of three living areas: the aft deck lounge that she'd already seen, the indoor galley and the most incredibly functional bedroom space ever. It took up the whole bow, filling the front of the *Portus* with panoramic, all-seeing windows, below which wrapped fitted black cupboards. She trailed a finger along the spotless black surface, over the part that was set up as a workspace, complete with expensive camouflaged laptop, hip-height bookshelves, a disguised mini-bar and a perfectly made up king-sized bed positioned centrally in the space, complete with black pillow and quilt covers. The whole space screamed sensuality and not just because of all the black.

A steamy kind of heat billowed up from under Mila's work shirt. It was way too easy to imagine Rich in here.

'Where's the widescreen TV?' she asked, hunting for the final touch to the space that she knew had to be here somewhere.

Rich leaned next to the workspace. 'I had it removed. When I'm in here it's not to watch TV.'

She turned to face him. 'Is that because this is an office first, or a bedroom first?'

The moments the words left her lips she tried to recapture them, horrified at her own boldness. It had to be the result of this all-consuming black making her skin tingle, but talking about a client's bedroom habits *with* said client was not just inappropriate, it was utterly mortifying.

'I'm so sorry...' she said hurriedly.

Rich held up a hand and the smile finally returned, lighting up the luxurious space.

'My own fault for having such a rock star bedroom,' he joked. 'I didn't buy the *Portus* for this space, but I have to admit it's pretty functional. Everything I need is close by. But who needs a TV when you have a wraparound view like this, right?'

She followed his easy wave out of the expansive windows. There was something just too...perfect about the image he created. And she just couldn't see him sitting still long enough to enjoy a view.

'You work when you're on board, don't you?'

Those coral-coloured lips twisted. 'Maybe.'

Mila hunted around for a topic of discussion that would soak up some of the cotton candy suddenly swilling around the room. 'Where do your crew sleep?'

The business of climbing down into one of the hulls, where a small bed space and washing facility were, gave her the time she needed to get her rogue senses back in order.

'…comfortable enough for short trips,' Rich was saying as she tuned back in.

'What about long ones?'

He glanced out of the window. 'WestCorp keeps me pretty much tethered to the city. This is shaping up to be the longest trip I've taken since I got her. Three days.'

Wow. Last of the big spenders.

'Come on.' He straightened, maybe seeing the judgement in that thought on her face. 'Let's finish the tour.'

The rest of the *Portus* consisted of a marble-clad *en suite* bathroom, appointed with the same kind of luxury as everywhere else, and then a trip back out to the aft deck and up a spiral staircase to the helm. Like everything else on the vessel, it was a wonder of compact efficiency. Buttons and LED panels and two screens with high-tech navigation and seafloor mapping and a bunch of other equipment she didn't recognise. The *Portus*' captain introduced himself but Mila stood back just far enough that a handshake would be awkward to ask for. She'd rather not insult a second man today. Maybe a third.

'Two crew?' she murmured. The vessel was large enough for it, but for just one passenger...?

'It's more efficient to run overnight. Tag-teaming the skippering. Get up from the city faster. I left the office at seven two nights ago and woke up here the next morning. Same deal tonight. I'll leave before sunset and be back in Perth just in time for my personal trainer.'

Imagine having a boat like this and then rushing every moment you were on her. This gorgeous vessel suddenly became relegated to a water taxi. Despite the wealth and comfort around her, she found herself feeling particularly sorry for Richard Grundy.

Captain Farrow pressed a finger to his headset and spoke quietly, then he turned to Rich.

'Lunch is served, sir.'

'Thanks, Max.'

They backtracked and found the sumptuous spread and the remainder of the wine set out on the aft deck. The deckhand known as Damo lowered his head respectfully then jogged on tanned legs up the spiral stairs to the helm and was gone.

Rich indicated for her to sit.

The first thing she noticed was the absence of the promised crayfish. In its place were some pieces of chicken. The little kindness touched her even as she wondered exactly how and when he'd communicated the instruction. Clearly, his crew had a talent for operating invisibly.

'This is amazing,' she said, curling her bare legs under her on the soft leather. The deep strains of wind chimes flew out of the back of the boat and were overwhelmed in the wash, but they endured. Mila loaded her small plate with delicious morsels.

'So how long have you worked for the Department?' Rich asked, loading a piece of sourdough with pâté and goat's cheese.

It wasn't unusual for one of her tour clients to strike up a personal conversation; what was unusual was the ease with which she approached her answer.

She normally didn't *do* chatty.

'Six years. Until I was eighteen, I instructed

snorkelers during the busy season and volunteered on conservation projects in the off-season.'

'While most other teens were bagging groceries or flipping burgers after school?'

'It's different up here. Station work, hospitality or conservation. Those are our options. Or leaving, of course,' she acknowledged. Plenty of young people chose that.

'Waiting on people not your thing?'

She studied her food for a moment. 'People aren't really my thing, to be honest. I much prefer the solitude of the reef system.'

It was the perfect *in* if he wanted to call her on her interpersonal skills. Or lack of.

But he didn't. 'What about working on the Station? Not too many people out there, I wouldn't have thought.'

'I would have worked on Wardoo in a heartbeat,' she admitted. 'But jobs there are very competitive and the size of their crew gets smaller every year as the owners cut back and back.' She looked out towards the vast rust-coloured land on their port side. 'And back.'

He shifted on the comfortable cushions as though he was perched on open reef flat.

'Vast is an understatement,' he murmured, following the direction of her eyes. And her thoughts.

That was not awe in his voice.

'Remote living is not for everyone,' she admitted, refocusing on him. 'But it has its perks.'

He settled back against the plush cushions but his gaze didn't relax with him. If anything, it grew more focused. More intense. 'Like what?'

'You can breathe up here,' she started, remembering how cloistered she'd felt on her one and only visit to the capital when she was a teen. 'The land sets the pace, not someone else's schedule. It's...predictable. Ordered.'

She forked up a piece of chicken and dipped it in a tangy sauce before biting into it and chewing thoughtfully.

'Some people would call that dull...' he started, carefully.

Meaning he would? 'Not me. Life has enough variability in it without giving every day a different purpose.'

'And that's important...why, exactly?'

His gaze grew keen. Too keen, as if he was poking around in a reef cave for something.

Oh...

She should have known he would notice. A man didn't get a boat like this—or the company that paid for it—without being pretty switched on. A deep breath lifted her shoulders before dropping them again. For a moment, Mila was disappointed that he couldn't just...let it lie. She understood the curiosity about her crossed senses, but all her life she'd just wanted someone to *not* be interested in her synaesthesia. So that she could feel normal for a moment.

Apparently, Richard Grundy wasn't going to be that someone.

She sighed. 'You're asking about...'

Funny how she always struggled to broach the subject. He helped her out.

'About crayfish with optimism and the smug reef.' She held her tongue, forcing him to go on. 'You seem very connected to the environment around you. I wondered if it was a cultural thing. Some affinity with your ancestors...?'

Was that what he thought? That it was *cultural*? Of all the things she'd ever thought were going on with her, it had truly never occurred to her that it had anything to do with being raised Bayungu. Probably because no one else on that side of the family had it—or any of the community.

It was just one more way that she was different.

'It's not affinity,' she said simply.

It was *her.*

'If anything, it probably comes from my Irish side. My grandmother ended up marrying a Japanese pearler because other people apparently found her—'

Unrelatable. Uncomfortable. Any of a bunch of other 'un's that Mila lived with too.

'Eccentric.'

But not Grandfather Hiro, with his enormous heart. A Japanese man in outback Australia during the post-war years would have known more than a little something about not fitting in. Pity he wasn't still around to talk to...

Rich laid his fork down and just waited.

'I have synaesthesia,' she blurted. 'So I hear some sensations. I taste and smell some emotions. Certain things have personalities.'

He kept right on staring.

'My synapses are all crossed,' she said in an attempt to clarify. Although even that didn't quite describe it.

'So…' Rich looked utterly confounded. '…the crayfish has an *actual* personality for you?'

'Yes. Kind of…perky.'

'All of them?'

'No. Just the dead one in your fridge.'

It was impossible not to ruin her straight face with a chuckle. Force of habit; she'd been minimising her condition with laughter for years. Trying to lessen the discomfort of others. Even if that meant taking it on herself. 'Yes, all of them, thank goodness. Things are busy enough without giving them *individual* traits.'

He sat forward. 'And the reef is actually—'

'Smug,' she finished for him. 'But not unpleasantly so. Sky, on the other hand, is quite conceited. Clouds are ambitious.' She glanced around at things she could see for inspiration. 'Your stainless steel fridge is pleasantly mysterious.'

He blinked. 'You don't like sky?'

'I don't like conceit. But I don't pick the associations. They just…are.'

He stared, then, so long and so hard she grew physically uncomfortable. In a way that had nothing to do with her synaesthesia and everything to do with the piercing intelligence behind those blue eyes.

Eventually his bottom lip pushed out and he conceded, 'I guess sky is kind of pleased with itself. All that over-confident blue…'

The candyfloss surged back for a half-moment and then dissipated on the air rushing past the boat. She was no less a spectacle but at least he was taking it in his stride, which wasn't always the case when she confessed her unique perception to people.

'What about the boat?' he asked after a moment. 'Or is it just natural features?'

Her lips tightened and she glanced down at the rapidly emptying platter. 'I'm not an amusement ride, Rich.'

'No. Sorry, I'm just trying to get my head around it. I've never met a…'

'Synaesthete.'

He tested the word silently on his lips and frowned. 'Sounds very sci-fi.'

'My brothers did call it my *superpower,* growing up.' Except that it wasn't terribly super and it didn't make her feel powerful. Quite the opposite, some days. 'I didn't even know that other people didn't experience the world like I did until I was about eleven.'

Before that, she'd just assumed she was flat-out unlikeable.

Rich dropped his eyes away for a moment and he busied himself topping up their glasses. 'So you mentioned sensation? Is that why you tensed up when you shook my hand?'

Heat rushed up Mila's cheeks. He'd noticed that? Had he also noticed every other reaction she'd had to being near him?

That could get awkward fast.

'Someone new might feel okay or they might… not.' She wasn't about to apologise for something that just…was…for her.

Rich studied her. 'Must be lonely.'

Her spine ratcheted straight. The only thing she wanted more than to be treated normally was *not* to be treated with pity. She took her time taking a long sip of wine.

'Are my questions upsetting you?'

'I don't… It's not something I usually talk about with strangers. Until I know someone well. People generally react somewhere on a spectrum from obsessive curiosity to outright incredulity.

No one's ever just shrugged and said, *All right, then. More sandwiches?*'

Oh, how she longed for that.

'Thank you for making an exception, then.' His eyes stayed locked on hers and he slid the platter slightly towards her. 'More sandwiches?'

It was so close, it stole her breath.

'Why are you really up here, Rich?' she asked, before thinking better of it. It shouldn't matter why; she was paid to show him the area, end of story. His business was as much his own as hers was. But something pushed her on. And not just the desire to change the subject. 'I'm going to look you up online anyway. Might as well tell me. Are you a developer?'

He shifted in his seat, took his time answering. 'You don't like developers, I take it?'

'I guide a lot of them. They spend the day banging on about their grand plans for the area and then I never see them again. I'm just wondering if you'll be the same.'

Not that she was particularly hoping to see him again. *Was she?*

His body language was easy but there was

an intensity in his gaze that she couldn't quite define.

'None of them ever come back?'

'Some underestimate how remote it is. Or how much red tape there will be. Most have no idea of the access restrictions that are in place.'

He tipped his head as he sipped his wine. 'Restrictions? Sounds difficult.'

'Technically,' she went on, 'the land all the way up to the National Park is under the control of three local pastoralists. Lifetime leaseholds. In Coral Bay, if anyone wants to get a serious foothold in this part of the Marine Park, they have to get past the Dawsons. No one ever has.' She shifted forward. 'Honestly, Rich? If you do have development plans, you might as well give up now.'

Why was she giving him a heads-up? Just because he'd been nice to her and given her lunch? And looked good in board shorts?

Blue eyes considered her closely. 'The Dawsons sound like a problem.'

The boiled eggs of loyalty materialised determinedly at the back of her throat. 'They're the reason the land around Coral Bay isn't littered with luxury resorts trying to position themselves on World Heritage coast. They're like a final rampart. Yet to be breached. That makes them heroes in my book.'

Rich studied her for a long time before lifting his glass in salute. And in thanks. 'To the Dawsons, then.'

Had she said too much? Nothing he probably didn't already know, or wouldn't find out soon enough. But still...

She ran her hands up and down arms suddenly bristling with goose pimples.

'Cold?' Rich asked, even though the sun was high.

Mila shook her head. 'Ball bearings.'

CHAPTER FOUR

RICH WANTED TO believe that 'ball bearings' referred to the breeze presently stirring wisps of long, dark hair around Mila's face, but what if she sensed ball bearings when she was feeling foreboding? Or deception. Or distrust.

What if she had more 'extra-sensory' in her 'super-sensory' than she knew? He *was* keeping secrets and she *should* feel foreboding. But that wasn't how Mila's condition worked. Not that he had much of an idea how it *did* work, and he didn't want to pummel her with curious questions just for his own satisfaction. He'd just have to use the brain his parents had spent a fortune improving to figure Mila out the old-fashioned way—through conversation.

A big part of him wished that the heroic Dawsons *were* an impediment to his plans—a good fight always got his blood up. But Mila would be dismayed to discover just how easy it was going to be for him to build his hotel overlooking the reef. The handful of small businesses running here might have had mixed feelings about the percentage that WestCorp took from their take—the motel, the café, the fuel station, even the hard-working glass-bottom boat tours—but they couldn't honestly expect not to pay for the privilege of running a business on Wardoo's land, just as Wardoo had to pay the government for the privilege of running cattle on leasehold land.

Money flowed like an ebbing tide towards the government. It was all part of the food chain.

Except now that same government was shifting the goalposts, looking to excise the coastal strip from the leasehold boundaries. The only part that made any decent profit. And his analysts agreed with him that the only way to get them to leave the lucrative coastal strip in the lease was to make a reasonable capital investment in the region himself—put something back in.

Governments liked to see potential leveraged and demand met.

And—frankly—he liked to do it.

WestCorp needed the lucrative coastal strip to supplement the Station's meagre profits. Without it, there was nothing holding Wardoo in any half-competent finance holdings and, thanks to his father's move to the big smoke forty years ago, there was nothing holding *him* to Wardoo. His heritage.

That was why he'd hauled himself out of the office—out of the city—and come north, to see for himself the place that had been earmarked for development. Just so he could be as persuasive as possible when he pitched it to the responsible bureaucrat. He'd lucked out with a guide who could also give him a glimpse of community attitudes towards his business—forewarned absolutely was forearmed.

It didn't hurt that Mila was such a puzzle—he'd always liked a challenge. Or that she was so easy on the eye. He'd always liked beautiful things. Now she was just plain intriguing too, courtesy of her synaesthesia. Though he'd have to temper his curiosity, given how touchy she was about it. Had someone made her feel like a freak in the past?

The *Portus'* motor cut out and they slowed to a drift. Mila twisted and stared at the ancient rocky range that stretched up and down the coast, red as far as they could see. She knew where they were immediately.

'We'll have to take the tender in; there's only a slim channel in the reef.'

It was narrow and a little bit turbulent where the contents of the reef lagoon rushed out into open water but they paused long enough to watch a couple of manta rays rolling and scooping just there, clearly taking advantage of the fishy freeway as they puttered over the top of it. Damo dropped them close enough to wade comfortably in, their shoes in one hand and sharing the load of the single kayak they'd towed in behind the tender in the other. They hauled it up to the sandbar that stretched across the mouth of Yardi Creek. Or once had.

'This is why we couldn't just drive up here,' she said, indicating the mostly submerged ridge. 'Thanks to a ferocious cyclone season earlier in the year, the sandbar blew out, taking the four-wheel drive access with it. It's only just now re-forming. It'll be good to go again at the end of the year but for now it makes for a convenient launch point for us.'

And launch they did. His sea kayak was wider

and flatter than a regular canoe, which made it possible for two of them to fit on a vessel technically designed for half that number. He slid down into the moulded seat well and scooted back to make room for Mila, spreading his legs along the kayak's lip so she could sit comfortably between them at the front of the seat well, with her own bent legs dangling over each side. Once she was in, he bent his knees up on either side of her to serve as some kind of amusement park ride safety barrier and unlocked his double paddle into a single half for each of them.

They soon fell into an easy rhythm that didn't fight the other, though Mila's body stayed as rigid and unyielding as the hard plastic of the kayak against his legs. Given what he now knew about her, this kind of physical contact had to be difficult for her. Not that she was snuggled up to him exactly, but the unconventional position wasn't easy for either of them. Though maybe for different reasons. *He* was supposed to be paying attention to everything around him yet he kept finding his gaze returning to the slim, tanned back and neck of the young woman seated between his knees, her now-dry ponytail hanging not quite neatly down her notched spine. She'd shrugged out of her uniform shirt and folded it neatly into her backpack but somehow—in this marine environment—the bikini top was as much of a uniform as anything.

She was in her mid-twenties—nearly a decade younger than he was—but there was something about her... As if she'd been here a whole lot longer. Born of the land, or even the sea. She just... belonged.

'Looks like we have the creek to ourselves.' Mila's soft words came easily back to him. courtesy of the gorge's natural acoustics.

Sure enough, there was not another human being visible anywhere—on the glassy water, up on the top of the massive canyon cliffs, in the car park gouged out of the limestone and dunes. Though it was easy to imagine a solitary figure, dark and mysterious, silhouetted against the sun, spear casually at hand, watching their approach far below.

It was just that kind of place.

Mila stopped paddling and he copied her, the drag of his paddle embedded in the water slowing them to almost nothing. Ahead, a pair of nostrils and a snub-nosed little face emerged from the water, blinking, checking them out. The kayak drifted silently past him on inertia. Only at the last moment did he dip back underwater and vanish to the depths of the deep canyon creek.

'Hawksbill turtle,' Mila murmured back to him once they were clear. 'Curious little guy.'

'You get curiosity for turtles?'

She turned half back, smiled. 'No. I mean he was *actually* curious. About us. I get bossy for turtles.'

They paddled on in silence. Rich battled with a burning question.

'Does it affect how you feel about some things?' he finally asked, as casually as he could. 'If your perception is negative?'

'It can.'

She didn't elaborate and he wondered if that question—or any question—held some hidden offence, but her voice when she finally continued wasn't tight.

'I'm not a huge fan of yellow fish, for instance, through no fault of their own. I read yellow as derisive and so...' She shrugged. 'But, similarly, people and things can strike me positively because of their associations too.'

'Like what?' he asked.

She paused again, took an age to answer. 'Oak moss. I used to get that when I was curled in my mother's arms as a child. I get it now when I'm wrapped up in my softest, woolliest sweater on a cold night, or snuggled under a quilt. It's impossible not to feel positive about oak moss.'

Her love came through loud and clear in her low voice and he was a bit sorry that he was neither naturally oaky nor mossy. It threw him back to a time, long ago, when he'd done the same with his own mother. Before he'd lost her at the end of primary school. Before he'd been dumped into boarding school by his not-coping father.

There'd been no loving arms at all after that.

She cleared her throat and kept her back firmly to him.

'Once, I met someone who registered as cotton candy. Hard not to respond positively to such a fun and evocative scent memory. I was probably more predisposed to like and trust him than, say, someone who I read as diesel smoke.'

Lucky cotton candy guy. Something told him

that being liked and trusted by Mila Nakano was rarer than the mysteries in this gorge.

'What's the worst association you've ever made?' Curious was as close to 'accepting' as she was going to let him get.

'Earwax,' she said softly.

'Was that a person or a thing?'

The kayak sent out ripples ahead of them but it was easy to imagine they were soundwaves from her laughter. It was rich and throaty and it got right in between his ribs.

'A person, unfortunately.' She sighed. 'The one kid at primary school that gave me a chance. Whenever they were around I got a strong hit of earwax in the back of my throat and nose. Now, whenever my heart is sad for any reason at all, I get a delightful reminder…'

Imagine trying to forge a friendship—or, worse, a relationship—with someone who struck you so negatively whenever they were around. How impossible it would be. How that would put you off experimenting with pretty much anyone.

Suddenly, he got a sense of how her superpower worked. He was going to find it difficult to go out on this kayak ever again without an image of Mila's lean, long back popping into his head. Or to watch ripples radiate on still water anywhere without hearing her soft voice. The only difference was that her associations didn't need to have a foundation in real life.

Mila dug the paddle hard into the water again and turned her face up and to the right as the kayak slowed. 'Black-flanked rock wallaby.'

Rich followed her gaze up the towering cliffs that lined both sides of the deep creek and hunted the vertical, rust-coloured rock face. 'All I see are some shadowy overhangs. What am I missing?'

'That's where the wallabies like to lurk. It's why they have evolved black markings.'

He scanned the sheer cliffs for camouflaged little faces. 'What are they, half mountain goat? Don't they fall off?'

'They're born up there, spend their lives leaping from claw-hold to claw-hold, nibbling on the plants that grow there, sleeping under the overhangs, raising their own young away from most predators. They're adapted to it. It's totally normal to them. They would be so surprised to know how impossible we find it.'

He fell back into rhythm with her gentle paddling. Was she talking about wallabies now or was she talking about her synaesthesia?

The more he looked, the more he saw, and the further he paddled, the more Mila showed him. She talked about the prehistoric-looking fish species that liked the cold, dark depths of the creek's uppermost reaches, the osprey and egrets that nested in its heights, the people who had once lived here and the ancient sites that were being rediscovered every year.

It was impossible not to imagine the tourist potential of building something substantial down the coast from a natural resource like this. An eco-resort in eco-central. Above them, small openings now occupied by wallabies hinted at so much more.

'The cavers must love it here,' he guessed. He knew enough about rocks to know these ones were probably riddled with holes.

'One year there was a massive speleologist convention and cavers from all over the world came specifically to explore the uncharted parts of the Range. They discovered nearly twelve new caves in two days. Imagine what they might have found if they could have stayed up here for a week. Or two!'

'Why couldn't they?'

'There just aren't any facilities up here to house groups of that size. Or labs to accommodate scientists or…really anything. Still, the caves have waited this long, I guess.' Her shoulders slumped. 'As long as the sea doesn't rise any faster.'

In which case the coastal range where the rock wallabies clung would go back to being islands and the exposed rock they were exploring would eventually be blanketed in corals again.

The circle of life.

They took their time paddling the crumbled-in end of the gorge, looking closely at the make-up of the towering walls, the same shapes he'd seen out on the reef here, just fossilised, the synchronised slosh of their oars the only sounds between them.

The silence in this beautiful place was otherwise complete. It soaked into him in a way he'd never really felt before and he finally understood why Mila might have thought that open ocean wasn't really that quiet at all.

Because she had *this* to compare it to.

'So, I'm thinking of coming back on the weekend,' he said when they were nearly done, before realising he'd even decided. 'For a couple more days. I've obviously underestimated what brings people here.'

They bumped back up against the re-establishing sand bar and Mila clambered out then turned to him with something close to suspicion on her pretty face. After the connection he thought they'd just made it was a disappointing setback.

'I'm only booked for today,' she said bluntly. 'You'll have to find someone else to guide you.'

Denial surged through him.

'You have other clients?' He could get that changed with one phone call. But pulling rank on her like that would be about as popular as... earwax.

'No, but I've got things on.'

'What kind of things?'

'An aerial survey of seagrasses and some whale shark pattern work. A tagging job. And the neap tide is this weekend so I'll be part of the annual spawn collection team. It's a big deal up here.'

Rich felt his chance at continuing to get quality

insider information—and his opportunity to get to know Mila a bit better—slipping rapidly away.

'Can I come along? Two birds, one stone.' Then, when she hesitated awkwardly, he added, 'Paid, of course.'

She winced. 'It's not about money. I'm just not sure whether that's okay. Most of our work isn't really a spectator sport.'

It was a practical enough excuse. But every instinct told him it was only half the truth. Was she truly so used to only ever seeing developers the one time? Well, he liked to be memorable.

'Put me to work, then. I can count seagrass or study the...spawn.'

Ten minutes ago that would have earned him another throaty laugh. Now, she just frowned.

'Come on, Mila, wasn't it you who asked when I'd last done something completely new to me? This is an opportunity. A bunch of new experiences.' He found the small tussle of wills disproportionately exhilarating. 'I'll be low-maintenance. Scout's honour.'

She shrugged as she bent to hike her side of the kayak up, but the lines either side of her flat lips told him she wasn't feeling that casual at all.

'It's your time to waste, I guess.'

He only realised he'd been holding his breath when he was able to let it out on a slow, satisfied smile. More time to get a feel for this district and more time to get his head around Mila Nakano.

The return trip felt as if it took half the time, as return trips often did. But it was long enough for Mila to carefully pick her way out to the front of the *Portus* and slide down behind the safety barrier on one of the catamaran hulls. Rich did the same on the other and—together but apart—they lost themselves in the deep blue ocean until they reached the open waters off Coral Bay again. Over on her side, the water whooshing past sang triumphantly.

Regardless, she shifted on the deck and let her shoulders slump.

She'd been rude. Even she could see that. Properly, officially rude.

But the moment Rich had decided to return to Coral Bay for a more in-depth look she'd felt a clawing kind of tension start to climb her spine. Coming back meant he wasn't a *one* any more. Coming back meant that none of the remoteness or the politics or the environmental considerations had deterred him particularly.

Coming back meant he was serious.

She'd guided Rich today because that was her job. But she'd let herself be disarmed by his handsome face and fancy boat and his apparently genuine interest in the reef and cape. Her only comfort was that he still had to get past the Dawsons—and no one had ever managed that—but she still didn't want him to think that she somehow endorsed his plans to develop the bay.

Whatever they were.

Regardless of the cautious camaraderie that had grown between them, Richard Grundy was still her adversary. Because he was the reef's adversary.

She cast her eyes across the deep green ocean flashing by below the twin hulls. Rich sat much as she did, legs dangling, spray in his face, but his gaze was turned away from her, his focus firmly fixed on the coast as they raced south parallel to it. No doubt visualising how his hotel was going to look looming over the water. Or his resort.

Or—perish the thought—his casino.

Knowing wouldn't change anything, yet she

had to work hard at not being obsessed by which it would be.

They met on the aft deck as the catamaran drew to an idling halt off Bill's Bay an hour later. Behind them, the sun was making fairly rapid progress towards the horizon.

'It was good to meet you,' she murmured politely, already backing away.

Rich frowned. 'You say that like I won't be seeing you again...'

The weekend was four days away. Anything could happen in that time, including him losing his enthusiasm for returning. Just because he was eager for it now didn't mean he'd still be hot for it after the long journey back to the city and his overflowing inbox. Or maybe she'd have arranged someone else to show him around on Saturday. That would be the smart thing to do. This could quite easily be the last she ever saw of Richard Grundy.

At the back of her throat the slightest tang began to climb over the smell of the ocean.

Earwax.

Which was ridiculous. Rich was virtually a stranger; why would her heart squeeze even a little bit at the thought of parting? But her senses never lied, even when she was lying to herself. That was unmistakably earwax she could taste.

Which made Saturday a really bad idea.

She hurried down to the dive platform on one of the *Portus'* hulls when Rich might have kissed her cheek in farewell, and she busied herself climbing aboard the tender when he might have offered her a helpful outstretched hand. But once she was aboard and the skipper began to throttle the tender out from under the *Portus* she had no real excuse—other than rudeness—not to look back at Rich, his hands shoved deeply into his pockets, still standing on the small dive platform. It changed the shape of his arms and shoulders below the T-shirt he'd put on when they'd got back aboard, showing off the sculpted muscles she'd tried so hard not to appreciate when they were snorkelling. Or when they brushed her briefly while they were paddling the kayak.

'Seven a.m. Saturday, then?' he called over the tender's thrum and nodded towards the marina. It would have sounded like an order if not for the three little forks between his blue eyes.

Doubt.

In a man who probably never second-guessed himself.

'Don't look for me,' she called back to him. 'Look for the uniform.' Just in case. Any one of her colleagues could show him the area.

She should have scrunched her nose as the tender reversed through a light fog of its own diesel exhaust, but all she could taste and smell in the back of her throat was candyfloss. The flavour she was rapidly coming to associate with Rich.

The flavour she was rapidly coming to crave like a sugary drug.

She was almost ashore before she realised that the presence of candyfloss in her mind's nose meant she'd already decided to be the one who met him on Saturday.

The first thing Mila did when she got back to her desk was jump online and check out the etymology of the word *portus*. She'd guessed Greek—some water god or something—but it turned out it was Latin...for port. *Duh!* But it also meant sanctuary, and the imposing vessel certainly was that—even up here, where everything around them was already nine parts tranquil. She'd felt it the moment she'd stepped aboard Rich's luxurious boat. She could only imagine what it was like for him to climb aboard and motor away from the busy city and his corporate responsibilities for a day or two.

No…only ever one. Hadn't he told her as much?

What were those corporate responsibilities, exactly?

It took only moments to search up WestCorp and discover how many pies the corporation had its fingers in. And a couple of media stories that came back high in the search results told her that Richard Grundy was the CEO of WestCorp and had been since the massive and unexpected heart attack that had taken his father. Rich had been carrying the entire corporation since then. No wonder he'd been on the phone a lot that morning. No wonder he didn't have time to use his boat. The Internet celebrated the growth of WestCorp in his few short years. There were pages of resource holdings and she lost interest after only the first few.

Suffice to say that Mr Richard Grundy was as corporate as they came.

Despite that, somewhere between getting off

the *Portus* and setting foot back on land she'd decided to definitely be the one to meet him on Saturday. Not just because of the candyfloss, which she reluctantly understood—biology was biology and even hers, tangled as it was with other input, was working just fine when it came to someone so high up on the Mila Nakano Secret Hotness Scale—but because of the earwax.

Her earwax couldn't be for Rich—she just didn't know him well enough—it had to be for the reef. For what a company like WestCorp could do to it. If she left him in the hands of anyone else, could she guarantee that they'd make it as abundantly clear as she would how badly this area did not need development? How it was ticking along just fine as it was?

Or should she only trust something that important to herself?

She reached for her phone.

'Hey, Craig, it's Mila…'

A few minutes later she disconnected her call, reassured that the pilot of Saturday's aerial survey could accommodate an extra body without compromising the duration of the flight. So that was Rich sorted; he would get to see a little more of the region he wanted to know about, and she…

She, what?

She'd bought herself another day or two to work on him and convince him exactly why this region didn't need his fancy-pants development. It happened to also be another day or two for Rich to discover how complicated she and her synaesthesia were to be around but, at the end of the day, the breathy anticipation of her lonely heart had to mean less than the sanctity and security of her beloved reef.

It just had to.

CHAPTER FIVE

'WE'RE MAPPING WHAT?' Rich asked into the microphone of the headset they each wore on Saturday morning as the little Cessna lifted higher and higher. Coasting at fifteen hundred feet was the only way to truly appreciate the size and beauty of the whole area.

Dugongs, Mila mouthed back, turning her face out towards a nook in the distant coast where the landforms arranged themselves into the kind of seagrass habitat that the lumbering animals preferred. 'Manatees. Sea cows.'

When he just blinked, she delved into her pocket, swiped through an overcrowded photo roll and then passed the phone back to him.

'Dugong,' she repeated. 'They feed on the seagrasses. They all but disappeared at the start of the century after a cyclone smothered the seagrasses with silt. The department has been monitoring their return ever since.'

She patted the sizeable camera that was fixed to the open window of the aircraft by two heavy-duty braces. 'Their main feeding grounds are a little south of here but more and more are migrating into these sensitive secondary zones. We're tracking their range to measure the viability of recovery from another incident like it.'

The more she impressed upon him the complexity of the environmental situation, the less likely he would be to go ahead with his plans, right? The more words like 'sensitive' and 'fragile' and 'rare' that she used, the harder development would seem up here. Either he would recognise the total lack of sense of developing such delicate coast or—at the very least—he would foresee how much red tape lay in his future.

It couldn't hurt, anyway.

Rich shifted over to sit closer to her window, as if her view was any more revealing than his. This close, she could smell him over the residual whiff of aviation fuel. Cotton candy, as always, but there was something else… Something she couldn't identify. It didn't ring any alarm bells; on the contrary, it made her feel kind of settled.

In a way she hadn't stopped feeling since picking him up at the marina after four days apart.

Right.

It felt right.

'Craig comes up twice a day to spot for the whale shark cruises,' she said to distract herself from such a worrying association. To keep her focus firmly on work. She nodded down at the four white boats waiting just offshore. 'If he isn't scheduled to take tourists on a scenic flight then I hitch a lift and gather what data I can while we're up here.'

'Opportunistic,' Rich observed.

'Like the wildlife.' She smiled.

Okay, so he hadn't technically earned the smile, but she was struggling not to hand them out like sweets. What was going on with her today? She hadn't gushed over Craig when she saw him again after a week.

They flew in a wide arc out over the ocean and Rich shifted back to his own window and peered out. Below, areas of darkness on the water might have been the shadow of clouds, reef or expansive seagrass beds.

'We're looking for pale streaks in the dark beds,' Mila said. 'That's likely to be a dugong snuffling its way along the seafloor, vacuuming up everything it finds. Where there's one, hopefully there'll be more.'

Until you saw it, it was difficult to explain—something between a snail's trail and a jet stream—but, as soon as you saw it, it was unmistakable in the bay's kaleidoscopic waters.

They flew lower, back and forth over the grasses, eyes peeled. When she did this, she usually kept her focus tightly fixed on the sea below, not only to spot an elusive dugong but also to limit the distracting sensory input she was receiving from everything else she could see in her periphery. Today, though, she was failing at both.

She'd never been as aware of someone else as she was with Rich up here. If he shuffled, she noticed. If he smiled, she felt it. If he spoke, she attended.

It was infuriating.

'Is that one?' Rich asked, pointing to a murky streak not far from shore.

'Sure is!' Mila signalled to Craig, who adjusted course and took them closer. She tossed a pair of binoculars at Rich and locked onto his eyes. 'Go you.'

Given the animal she was supposed to be fascinated by, it took her a worryingly long time to tear her eyes away from Rich's and focus on the task at hand.

Through the zoom lens of her camera it was possible to not only get some detail on the ever-increasing forage trail of a feeding dugong but to also spot three more rolling around at the surface enjoying the warmest top layer of the sea and the rising sun. Her finger just about cramped on the camera's shutter release and she filled an entire memory card with images. Maybe a dozen or so would be useful to the dugong research team but until she got back to her office she couldn't know which. So she just kept shooting.

Rich shook his head as they finished up the aerial survey. 'Can't believe you get paid to do this.'

'Technically, I don't,' Mila admitted. 'I'm on my own time today.'

He turned a frown towards her and spoke straight into her ear, courtesy of the headsets. 'That doesn't seem right.'

She looked up at him. 'Why? What else would I do with the time?'

'Uh... Socialise? Sleep in? Watch a movie?'

'This is plenty social for my liking.' She chuckled, looking between Craig and Rich. 'And why watch a movie when I can be watching dugongs feeding?'

'So you never relax? You're always doing something wildlifey?'

His judgement stung a little. And not only because it was true. 'Says the man who has an office set up on his boat so he doesn't miss an email.'

'I run a *Fortune 100* company.' He tsked. 'You're just—'

'Dude...!' Craig choked out a warning before getting really busy flying the plane. All those switches that needed urgent flipping...

'Just?' Mila bristled, as the cabin filled with the unmissable scent of fried chicken. 'Is that right?'

But he was fearless.

'Mila, one of the few advantages to being an employ*ee* and not an employ*er* is that you get to just...switch off. Go home and not think about work until Monday.'

Wow. How out of touch with ordinary people was he?

'My job title may not be comprised of initials, Rich, but what I do is every bit as important and *as occupying* as what you do. The only difference is that I do it for the good of the reef and not for financial gain.'

Craig shook his head without looking back at either of them.

'I'm out,' she thought she heard him mutter in the headset.

Rich ignored him. 'Oh, you're some kind of philanthropist? Is that it?'

'How many voluntary hours did *you* complete last month?'

His voice crept up, even though the microphone at his throat meant it didn't need to. 'Personally? None; I don't have the time. But WestCorp has six new staff working for us in entry level roles who were homeless before we got to them and that's an initiative *I* started.'

Mila's outrage snapped shut.

'Oh.' She puffed out a breath. 'Well… That's not on your website.'

'You think that's something I should be splashing around? Exposing those people to public scrutiny and comment?'

No, that would be horrible. But would a corporation generally care about that when there was good press to be had?

The Cessna's engines spluttered on.

'So you made good on your threat to check up on me, I see,' he eventually queried, his voice softening.

Sour milk mingled in with the bitter embarrassment of Brussels sprouts for a truly distasteful mix. Though she was hardly the only uncomfortable one in the plane. Rich looked wary and Craig looked as if he wanted to leap out without wasting time with a parachute.

'I was just curious about what you did,' she confessed.

'Find anything interesting?'

'Not really.' But then she remembered. 'I'm sorry about your father.'

The twitch high in his clenched jaw got earwax flowing again and this time it came with a significant, tangible and all too actual squeeze behind her breast. Had she hurt him with her clumsy sympathy?

But he didn't bite; he just murmured, 'Thank you.'

The silence then was cola-flavoured and she sank into the awkwardness and chewed her lip as she studied the ocean below. Craig swung the plane around and headed back towards Coral Bay.

'Okay, we're on the clock,' he said, resettling in his seat, clearly relieved to have something constructive to say. 'Whale sharks, here we come.'

Rich knew enough about this region to know what it was most famous for—the seasonal influx of gentle giants of the sea. Whale sharks. More whale than shark, the massive fish were filter feeders and, thus, far safer for humans than the other big sharks also out there. Swimming out in the open waters with any of them was a tightly regulated industry and a massive money-spinner.

But, frankly, anyone doing it for fun had to be nuts.

The water was more than beautiful enough from up here without needing to be immersed in it and all its mysteries.

'What do you need with whale sharks?' he asked, keen to undo his offence of earlier with some easier conversation.

Mila couldn't know how secretly he yearned to be relieved of the pressure of running things, just for a while. A week. A weekend even. He hadn't had a weekend off since taking over WestCorp six years before. Even now, here, he was technically on the job. Constantly thinking, constantly assessing. While other people dreamed of fancy cars and penthouse views, his fantasies were a little more…*suburban.* A sofa, a warm body to curl around and whatever the latest hit series was on TV.

Downtime.

Imagine that.

He couldn't really name the last time he'd done something just for leisure. Sport was about competitiveness, rock-climbing was about discipline and willpower. If he read a book it was likely to be the autobiography of someone wildly successful. It was almost as if he didn't *want* to be alone. Or quiet. Or thoughtful.

So when he'd commented on Mila's downtime, he hadn't meant it as a criticism. Of everything he'd seen in Coral Bay so far, the thing that had made the biggest impression on him was the way Mila spent her days.

Spectacularly simple. While also being very full.

She patted her trusty camera.

'Whale sharks can be identified by their patterning rather than by invasive tagging. The science employs the same algorithms NASA uses to chart star systems.'

A pretty apt analogy. The whale sharks he'd seen in photos were blanketed in constellations of pale spots on a Russian blue skin.

Mila turned more fully to him and her engagement lit up her face just like one of those distant suns he saw as a star. It almost blinded him with optimism. 'Generally, the research team uses crowd-sourced images submitted by the tourists that swim with them but I try and contribute when I can.'

'You can photograph them from up here?'

'Oh, we'll be going lower, mate,' Craig said, over the rattle of the Cessna's engine. 'We're looking for grey tadpoles at the surface. Shout out if you see any.'

Tadpoles? From up here? He looked at Mila.

Her grin was infectious. 'You'll see.'

He liked to do well at things—that came from results-based schooling, an all-honours university career, and a career where he was judged by his successes—so he was super-motivated to replicate his outstanding dugong-spotting performance. But this time Mila was the first to spot a cluster of whale sharks far below.

'On your left, Craig.'

They banked and the sharks came into view.

'Tadpoles,' Rich murmured. Sure enough: square-nosed, slow-swimming tadpoles far, far below. 'How big are they?'

'Maybe forty feet,' Mila said. 'A nice little posse of three.'

'That'll keep the punters happy,' Craig said and switched channels while he radioed the location of the sharks in to the boats waiting patiently but blindly below.

'We'll stay with this pod until the boats get here,' Mila murmured. 'Circle lower and get our shots while we wait.'

Craig trod a careful line between getting Mila the proximity she needed and not scaring the whale sharks away into deeper waters. He descended in a lazy circle, keeping a forty-five-degree angle to the animals at all times. While Mila photographed their markings, Rich peered down through the binoculars to give him the same zoomed-in views she was getting. Far below, the three mammoth fish drifted in interlocking arcs, their big blunt heads narrowing down into long, gently waving tail fins. As if the tadpoles were moving in slow motion. There was an enviable kind of ease in their movements, as if they had nowhere better to be right now. No pressing engagements. No board meeting at nine. No media pack at eleven.

Hard not to envy them their easy life.

'The plankton goes down deep during the day so the whale sharks take long rests up here before going down to feed again at dusk,' Mila said. 'That's why they're so mellow with tourists, because they have a full belly and are half asleep.'

'How many are there on the whole reef?'

'Right now there's at least two dozen and more arriving every day because they're gathering for the coral spawn this weekend.'

'They eat the spawn?'

'Everyone eats the spawn. It's why the entire reef erupts all on the same night—to increase the chances of survival.' She glanced back at him. 'What?'

'You're pretty impressed with nature, aren't you?'

'I appreciate order,' she admitted. 'And nothing is quite as streamlined as evolution. No energy wasted.'

If his world was as cluttered as hers—with all her extrasensory input—he might have a thing for order too. His days tended to roll out in much the same way day in, day out.

Same monkeys, different circus.

'If it was just about systems you'd be happy working in a bank. Why out here? Why wildlife?'

She gave the whale sharks her focus but he knew he had her attention and he could see her thinking hard about her answer—or whether or not to give it to him, maybe. Finally, she slipped the headset off her head, glanced at an otherwise occupied Craig and leaned towards him. He met her in the middle and turned his ear towards her low voice.

'People never got me,' she said, low. And painfully simple. He got the sense that maybe this wasn't a discussion she had very often. Or very easily. 'Growing up. Other kids, their parents. They didn't hate me but they didn't accept me either, because I saw or heard or smelled things that they couldn't. Or they thought I was lying. Or making fun of them. Or defective. One boy called me "Mental Mila" and it kind of...stuck.'

Huh. He'd never wanted to punch a kid so much in his life.

'I already didn't fit anywhere culturally, then I discovered I didn't fit socially.' She looked down at the reef. 'Out there every species is as unique and specialised as the one next to it yet it doesn't make them exclusive. If anything, it makes them inclusive; they learn to work their specialties in together. Nature cooperates; it doesn't judge.'

Mankind sure did.

She slid the headset back on, returned to her final photos and the moment—and Mila's confidence—passed. He could so imagine her as a pretty, lonely young girl who turned her soft heart towards the non-judgemental wildlife and made them her friends.

The sorrowful image sucked all the joy out of his day.

The Cessna kept on circling the three-strong pod of whale sharks, keeping track of them until the boats of tourists began to converge, then Craig left them to their fun and scoured up the coast for a back-up group in case those ones decided to dive deep. As soon as they found more and radioed the alternate location, their job was done and Craig turned for Coral Bay's airfield, charting a direct line down the landward side of the coast.

As they crossed back over terra firma, Rich peered through the dusty window of his door at the red earth below. He knew that land more for its features on a map than anything else. The distinctive hexagonal dam that looked like a silver coin from here, but was one of the biggest in the region from the ground. The wagon wheel of stock tracks leading to it. The particular pattern of eroded ridges in Wardoo's northwest quadrant. The green oasis of the waterhole closer to the homestead. When he was a boy he'd accompanied his father on a charter flight over the top of the whole Station and been arrested by its geometry. For a little while he'd had an eight-year-old's fantasies of the family life he might have had there, as a kid on the land with a dozen brothers and sisters, parents who sat around a table at night, laughing, after a long day mustering stock...

'That's the Station I told you about,' Mila murmured, misreading his expression as interest.

'Wardoo isn't just beautiful coastline; its lands are spectacular too. All those fierce arid ripples.'

Fierce. He forced his mind back onto the present. 'Is that what you feel when you look at the Station?'

It went some way to explaining her great faith in Wardoo as a protector of the realm if looking at it gave her such strong associations.

'Isolation,' she said. 'There's an undertone in Wardoo's red…I get the same association with jarrah. Like the timber deck on your boat. It's lonely, to me.'

He stared down at all that red geometry. Fantasy Rich and his enormous fantasy family were pretty much all that had got him through losing his mother and then being cast off in boarding school. But by the time he was old enough to consider visiting by himself, he had no reason and even less time to indulge the old crutch. He'd created a stable, rational world for himself at school and thrown himself into getting the grades he needed to get into a top university. Once at uni he'd been all about killing it in exams so that he could excel in the company he'd been raised to inherit. He'd barely achieved that when his father's heart had suddenly stopped beating and, since then, he'd been all about taking WestCorp to new and strictly governable heights. There'd been very little time for anything else. And even less inclination.

Thus, maps and the occasional financial summary were his only reminder that Wardoo even existed.

Until now.

'Actually, I can see that one.'

Her eyes flicked up to his and kind of...crashed there. As if she hadn't expected him to be looking at her. But she didn't look away.

'Really?' she breathed.

There was an expectation in her gaze that stuck in his gut like a blade. As if she was hunting around for someone to understand her. To connect with.

As if she was ravenous for it.

'For what it's worth, Mila,' Rich murmured into the headset, 'your synaesthesia is the least exceptional thing about you.'

Up front, Craig's mouth dropped fully open, but Mila's face lit up like a firework and her smile grew so wide it almost broke her face.

'That's so lovely of you to say,' she breathed. 'Thank you.'

No one could accuse him of not knowing people. And people the world over all wanted the same thing. To belong. To fit. The more atypical that people found Mila, the less comfortable she was bound to be with them. And, even though it was a bad idea, he really wanted her to be comfortable with him for the few short hours they would have together. He turned and found her eyes—despite the fact that his voice was feeding directly to her ears courtesy of the headphones—and pumped all the understanding he could into his gaze.

'You're welcome.'

The most charged of silences fell and Craig was the only one detached enough to break it.

'Buckle up,' he told them both. 'Airstrip's ahead.'

Mila shifted towards the open door of the Cessna, where Rich had just slid out under its wing. As long as his back was to her she was fine, but the moment he turned to face her she knew she was in trouble. Normally she would have guarded against the inevitable barrage of crossed sensations that being swung down bodily by someone would bring. But, in his case, she had to steel herself against the pleasure—all that hard muscle and breadth against her own little body.

Tangled sensations had never felt so good.

Twenty-four hours ago she would have found some excuse to crawl through to the other door and exit far away from Rich, or accepted his hand—*maybe*—and limit the physical skin-on-skin to just their fingers, but now... She rested her hands lightly on his shoulders and held her breath. He eased her forward, over the edge of the door, and supported her as she slid his full length until her toes touched earth. Even then he didn't hurry to release her and the hot press of his body sent her into a harpy, sugary overdrive.

Your synaesthesia is the least exceptional thing about you.

To have it not be the first thing someone thought about when they thought about her... The novelty of that was mind-blowing. And it begged the question—what *did* he associate first with her? Not something she could ever ask for shame; ridiculous to be curious about and dangerous to want, given what he did for a living.

But there it was. As uncontrollable and illogical as her superpower. And she'd learned a long time ago to accept the inevitability of those.

Her nostrils twitched as her feet found purchase on the runway; alongside the usual carnival associations there was something else. Some indefinable...closeness. She felt inexplicably drawn to Richard Grundy. She'd been feeling it all morning.

It took a moment for her to realise.

She spun on him, eyes wide. 'What are you wearing?'

He didn't bother disguising his grin. He reached up with one arm and hooked it over the strut holding the Cessna's wing and fuselage to each other. The casual pose did uncomfortable things to her pulse.

'Do you have any idea how hard it is to find a cologne with oak moss undertones on short notice?' he said.

Mila stared even as her chest tightened. 'You wore it intentionally?'

'Totally. Unashamedly,' he added, as the gravity of her expression hit him. 'I wasn't sure it was working. You seemed unaffected at first.'

That was because she was fighting the sensation to crawl into his lap in the plane and fall asleep there.

Oak moss.

'Why would you do that?' she half whispered, thinking about that murmured discussion without their headsets. The things she'd confessed. The access she'd given him into her usually protected world.

He shrugged the shoulder that wasn't stretched up towards the plane's wing. 'Because you associate it with security.'

She fought back the rush of adrenaline and citrus that he'd cared at all how she felt around him and gave her anger free rein. 'And you thought manipulating the freak would somehow make me feel safe with you?'

He lowered his arm and straightened, his comfortable expression suddenly growing serious. 'Whoa, no, Mila. That's not what—'

'Then what? Why do I need to feel safe with you?'

She'd not seen Rich look anything but su-

premely confident since he'd first come striding towards her with his hand outstretched at
Nancy's Point. Now he looked positively bewil-
dered. And a little bit sick. It helped ease the
whiff of nail varnish that came with the devas-
tation.

This whole conversation stank more than an
industrial precinct.

'Because you're so wary and I...' He greyed
just a little bit more as his actions dawned on
him. 'Oh, God, Mila—'

'Way to go, bro!' Craig called as he breezed
past them with a hand raised in farewell and
marched towards the little shed that served as
the airfield's office.

Rich was way too fixated on her face to acknowledge his departure, but it bought them both
a moment to take a breath and think. Mila fought
her natural inclination to distrust.

Richard Grundy was not a serial killer. He
hadn't just spiked her drink in a nightclub. He
wasn't keeping strangers locked up in a base-
ment somewhere.

He'd worn something he thought would make
her comfortable around him.

That was all.

Mila could practically see his mind whirring away in that handsome head. He dropped his gaze to the crushed limestone runway and when it came back up his eyes were bleak. But firm. And she registered the truth in them.

'I wanted to ask you to dinner,' he admitted, low. 'And I wanted you to feel comfortable enough around me to say yes.'

'Do I look comfortable?'

He sagged. 'Not even a little bit.'

But every shade paler Rich went helped with that. He saw his mistake now and something told her that he very rarely made them. Old habits died hard, yet something in his demeanour caused a new and unfamiliar sensation to shimmer through her tense body.

Trust.

She wanted to believe in him.

'Why would you care whether I come to dinner or not?' Which was coward-speak for, *Why do you want to have dinner at all?*

With me.

'You intrigue me,' he began. 'And not because of the synaesthesia. Or not *just* because of it,' he added when she lifted a sceptical brow. 'I just wanted to get to know you better. And I wanted you to get to know *me* better.'

'I'm not sure you improve on repeat exposure, to be honest.'

Conflict shone live in his intense gaze. He battled it for moments. Then he decided.

'You know what? This was a mistake. *My* mistake,' he hurried to clarify.

'Big call from a man who never makes mistakes.'

His laugh was half-snort. And barely even that.

'Apparently, I save them up to perpetrate in one stunning atrocity.' His chest broadened with one breath. 'I succeed in business because of my foresight. My planning. Because I anticipate obstacles and plan for them. But I'm completely out of my depth with you, Mila. I have no idea where the boundaries are, never mind how I can control them. But that's a poor excuse for trying to game you.' He stepped out from under the shade of the Cessna's wing. 'Thank you for everything you've shown me and I wish you all the best for the future.'

He didn't try and shake her hand, or to touch

her in any way. He just delivered an awkward half-bow like some lord of a long-ago realm and started to back away. But at the last moment he stopped and turned back.

'I meant what I said, Mila, about you being exceptional for a whole bunch of reasons that have nothing to do with your synaesthesia. There's something about how you are on that reef, in this place…I think you and your super-connectedness to the world might just hold the secret to life. I don't understand it, but I'm envious as hell and I think I was just hoping that some of it might rub off on me.'

He nodded one last time and strode away.

A slam of freshly made toast hit her. *Sorrow.* Rich was saying goodbye just as she'd finally got to meet the real him. Just as he'd dropped his slick veneer and let her in through those aquamarine eyes—the colour that always energised her. She would never again know the harp strains of his touch, or the coffee of his easy company or the sugar-rush of his sexy smile. He would be just like every other suited stranger she'd ever guided up here.

A *one*.

She wasn't ready to assign him to those dreaded depths just yet. And not just because of the rapidly diminishing oak moss that made her feel so bereft. She'd spent her life being distanced by people and here was a man trying to close that up a little and she'd gone straight for the jugular.

Maybe she needed to be party to the distance-closing herself.

Maybe change started at home.

'Wait!'

She had to call it a second time because Rich had made such long-legged progress away from her. He stopped and turned almost as he stepped off the airfield onto the carefully reticulated grass that lined it. Some little voice deep down inside urged her that once he'd stepped onto that surface it would have been too late, that he'd have been lost to her.

That she'd caught something—barely—before it was gone for ever. 'What about the coral spawn?'

He frowned and called back. 'What about it?'

'You can't leave before you've seen it, surely? Having come all this way.'

His face grew guarded and she got toast again

as she realised that she'd made him feel as bad about himself as others had always made her feel.

'Is it that spectacular?' he called back warily.

'It's a miracle,' she said, catching up. Puffing slightly. More aware of someone than ever before in her life. 'And it should start tonight.'

He battled silently with himself again, and she searched his eyes for signs of an angle she just couldn't find.

'It would be my first miracle...' he conceded.

'And the moon has to be high to trigger it so, you know, we could grab something to eat beforehand.' She huffed out a breath. 'If you want.'

His smile, when it came, was like a Coral Bay sunrise. Slow to start but eye-watering when it came up over the ridge. It was heralded by a tsunami of candyfloss.

'That won't be weird? After...' He nodded towards the plane.

Cessna-gate?

'No,' she was quick to confirm. 'It wasn't the brightest thing you've done but I believe that you meant no harm.'

His handsome face softened with gratitude. But there was something else in there too, a shadow...

'Okay then,' he said, pushing it away. 'I'll meet you at the marina at six?'

Her breath bunched up in her throat like on-lookers crowding around some spectacle. It made it hard to say much more than, 'Okay.'

It was only at the last moment that she remembered to call out.

'Bring your fins!'

CHAPTER SIX

RICH BRACED HIS feet in the bottom of the tender as it puttered up to the busy pier, then leapt easily off onto the unweathered timbers without Damo needing to tie up amongst the dozen boaters also coming ashore for the evening.

Mila had been on his mind since he'd left her earlier in the day, until the raft of documents waiting for him had forced her out so that he could focus on the plans.

I believe that you meant no harm, she'd said.

Purposefully wearing one of her synaesthesia scents was only a small part of the hurt he feared he might be gearing up to perpetrate on this gentle creature. A decent man would have accepted another guide, or gone back to the city and stayed there. Made the necessary decisions from afar. A decent man wouldn't be finding reasons to stay close to Mila even as he did the paperwork that would change her world for ever. A driven man would. A focused man would.

He would.

Was there no way to succeed up here *and* get the girl?

Deep down, he knew that there probably wasn't.

Mila wouldn't be quite so quick to declare her confident belief in him if she knew that he had the draft plans for a reef-front resort sitting on his desk on board the *Portus*. Or why he was so unconcerned about any eleventh-hour development barriers from the local leaseholders.

Because he *was* that final barrier.

He *was* Wardoo.

And Wardoo's lease was up for renewal right now. There was no time to come up with another strategy, or for long-winded feasibility testing. *Someone* was going to develop this coast—him, the government, some offshore third party—and if he didn't act, then he would lose the coastal strip or the lease on Wardoo. Possibly both.

Then where would Mila and her reef be?

Better the devil and all that.

He waved Damo off and watched him putter past incoming boats, back out towards the *Portus*' holding site beyond the reef. As the sun sank closer to the western horizon, it cast an orange-yellow glow over everything, reflected perfectly in the still, mirrored surface of the windless lagoon. Did Mila dislike golden sunsets the way she distrusted yellow fish? He couldn't imagine her disliking anything about this unique place.

'Beautiful, isn't it,' a soft voice said behind him. 'I could look at that every day.'

Rich turned to face Mila, standing on the marina. He wanted to comment that she *did* look at it every day but the air he needed to accomplish it escaped from his lungs as soon as he set eyes on her.

She wasn't wet, or bedraggled, or crunchy-haired. She wasn't in uniform. Or in a bikini. Or any of the ways he'd seen her up until now. She stood, weight on one leg, hands twisted in front of her, her long dark hair hanging smooth and combed around her perfectly made-up face. All natural tones, almost impossible to see except that he'd been remembering that face without its make-up every hour of the day since he'd left on Tuesday and comparing it subconsciously to every other artfully made-up female face he'd seen since then. That meant he could spot the earthy, natural colours, so perfect on her tanned skin. A clasp of shells tightly circled her long throat while a longer strand hung down across the vee of smooth skin revealed by her simple knitted dress, almost the same light brown as her skin. The whole thing was held up by the flimsiest of straps, lying over the bikini she wore underneath. She looked casual enough to walk straight out into the glassy water, or boho enough to dine in any restaurant in the city. Even the best ones.

'Mila. Good to see you again.' *Ugh, that was formal.* He held up the snorkelling gear he'd purchased on his way back to the *Portus* that morning. 'Fins.'

Her smile seemed all the brighter in the golden light of evening and some of the twist in her fingers loosened up. 'I thought you might have left them on the boat by-accident-on-purpose. To get out of tonight.'

'Are you kidding? Miss out on such a unique event?'

She chewed her lip and it was adorable. 'I should confess that not everyone finds mass spawning as beautiful as I do.'

'Seriously? A sea full of floating sex cells. What's not to love?'

She stood grinning at him long enough for him to realise that he was standing just grinning at her too.

Ridiculous.

'Want me to drive?' he finally managed to say. 'It's such a long way.'

His words seemed to break Mila's trance and her laugh tinkled. 'I think I can handle it.'

He rolled around in that laugh, luxuriating, and his mind went again to the stack of plans on his desk.

Jerk.

It only took three minutes to drive around into the heart of Coral Bay. On the way, she asked him about his day at large in town and he asked her about hers. They filled the three minutes effortlessly.

And then they ran flat out of easy conversation.

As soon as they stepped out of her four-wheel drive in front of the restaurant, Mila's body seemed to tighten up. Was she anticipating the sensory impact of sharing a meal with dozens of others, or the awkwardness of sharing a meal with him? Whichever, her back grew rigid as her hand lifted to push the door open.

'Would it be crazy to suggest eating on the beach instead?' he asked before the noise from the restaurant reached more fully out to them. 'The lagoon is too beautiful not to look at to-night.'

As was Mila.

And he didn't really feel like sharing her with a restaurant full of people.

He watched her eagerness to seek the solace of the beach wrestle with her reluctance to be so alone with him. After what he'd pulled earlier, who could blame her? Sharing a meal in a crowded restaurant was one thing; sharing it on a moonlit beach made it much harder to pretend this was all just…business.

'I'm scent-free tonight,' he assured her, holding his hands out to his sides. Trying to keep it light.

'If only,' he thought he heard her mutter.

But then she spoke louder. 'Yes, that would be great; let's order to go.'

And go they did, all of one hundred metres down to the aptly named Paradise Beach, which stretched out expansively from the parking area.

The tide was returning but, still, the beach was wide and white and virtually empty. A lone man ran back and forth with a scrappy terrier, white sand flying against the golden sunset. The dog barked with exuberant joy.

'This looks good,' Rich said, unfolding the battered fish and potato scallops.

'Wait until you taste it,' she promised as the man and dog disappeared up a sandy track away from the beach. 'That fish was still swimming a couple of hours ago. They source locally and daily.'

Talking about food was only one step removed from talking about the weather and it almost pained him to make such inane small talk when his time with Mila was so limited.

He wanted to see the passion in her eyes again.

'Speaking of swimming, why exactly are we heading out into spawn-infested waters?' he encouraged. 'More volunteering?'

'This one's work-related. My whole department heads out at different points of the Northwest Cape on the first nights of the eruption to collect spawn. So we have diverse genetic stock.'

'For what?'

'The spawn bank.'

He just blinked. 'There's a spawn *bank*?'

'There is. Or…there will be, one day. Right now it's a locked chest freezer in Steve Donahue's fish shed, but some day the fertilised spawn will help to repopulate this reef if it's destroyed. Or we can intentionally repopulate individual patches that die off.' She turned to him, her eyes glowing as golden as the sunset. 'Tonight we collect and freeze, and in the future they'll culture and release the resulting embryos to wiggle their way back onto the reef and fix there.'

'That sounds—' *Desperate? A lost cause?* '—ambitious.'

'We have to do something.' She shrugged. 'One outbreak of disease or a feral competitor, rising global temperatures or a really brutal cyclone… All of that would be gone.'

His eyes followed hers out to the darkening lagoon and the reef no longer visible anywhere above it. The water line was nearly twice as far up the beach as it had been when the *Portus* set him ashore. He didn't realise there were so many threats to the reef's survival.

Threats that didn't include him, anyway.

'And how do you know it will be tonight?'

'It's usually triggered by March's full moon.'

He glanced up at the crescent moon peeking over the eastern horizon. 'Shouldn't you have done this last week, then?'

'By the time they've grown for ten days, the moonlight is dim enough to help hide the spawn bundles from every other creature on the reef waiting to eat them.' She glanced out to the horizon. 'It will probably be more spectacular tomorrow night but I like to be in the water for the first eruptions. Not quite so soupy.'

'Sounds delicious,' he drawled.

But it didn't deter his enjoyment of his seafood as he finished it up.

'How far out are we going this time?'

He hated exposing himself with that question but he also liked to be as prepared as possible for challenges, including death-defying ones. Preparedness was how you stayed alive—in the boardroom and on the beach. There was nothing sensible about swimming out onto a reef after dark.

He'd seen the documentaries.

'The species we're after are all comfortably inside the break.'

Comfortably. Nothing about this was comfortable. It was testament to how badly he wanted to be with Mila that he was entertaining the idea at all.

They fell to silence and talked about nothing for a bit, Mila glancing now and again out to the lagoon to check that the spawning hadn't commenced while they were making small talk.

'Can I ask you something?' she eventually said, bringing her eyes back to him. 'How come the captain of the swim team doesn't like water? And don't mention your jet ski,' she interrupted as he opened his mouth. 'I'm talking about being *in* water.'

Given how she'd opened herself up to him about her synaesthesia, not returning the favour felt wrong. Yet going down this path scarcely felt any better, because of where he knew it led. And how she might judge him for that.

'I'm hurt that you've forgotten our first snorkel already…'

Her green eyes narrowed at his evasion.

He leaned forward and rested his elbows on his

knees. 'I like to be the only species in the water. Swimming pools are awesome for that.'

'Spoken like a true axial predator. You don't like to share?'

'Only child,' he grunted. But Mila still wasn't satisfied. That keen gaze stayed locked firmly on his until he felt obliged to offer up more. 'I like to know what I'm sharing with.'

'You know there's more chance of being killed by lightning than a shark, right?'

'I'd like to see those odds recalculated in the middle of an electrical storm.' Which was effectively what swimming out into their domain was like. Doubly so at night. On a reef.

He could stop there. Leave Mila thinking that he was concerned about sharks. Or whales. Or Jules Verne–type squid. She looked as if she was right on the verge of believing him. But he didn't want to leave her with that impression. Sharks and whales and squid mattered to Mila. And it mattered to *him* what she thought.

He sighed. 'Open ocean is not somewhere that mankind reigns particularly supreme.'

'Ah…' Awareness glowed as bright as the quarter-moonlight in Mila's expression. 'You can't control it.'

'I don't expect to,' he pointed out. 'It's not mine to control. I'm just happier not knowing what's down there.'

'Even if it's amazing?'

Especially if it was amazing. He was better off not knowing what he was missing. Wasn't that true of all areas of life? It certainly helped keep him on track at WestCorp—the only times he wobbled from the course he'd always charted for himself was when he paused to consider what else might be out there for him.

'As far as I'm concerned, human eyes can't see through ocean for a reason. Believing that it's all vast, empty nothing fits much better with my understanding of the world.'

Though that wasn't the world that Mila enjoyed, and it had nothing to do with her superpower.

'It is vast,' she acknowledged carefully. 'And you've probably become accustomed to having things within your power.'

'Is that what you think being CEO is about? Controlling things?'

'Isn't it?'

'It's more like a skipper. Steering things. And I've worked my whole life towards it.'

'You say that like you were greying at the temples when you stepped up. What are you now, mid-thirties? You must have been young when it happened.'

He remembered the day he'd got the call from the hospital, telling him about his father. Telling him to come. The sick feeling of hitting peak-hour traffic. The laws he'd broken trying to get there in time. Wishing for lights or sirens or *something* to help him change what was so obviously happening.

His father was dying and he wasn't there for it.

It was his mother all over again. Except, this time, he couldn't disappear into a child's fantasy world to cope.

'Adult enough that people counted on me to keep things running afterwards.'

'Was it unexpected?' she murmured.

'It shouldn't have been, the way he hammered the liquor and the cigarettes. The double espressos so sweet his spoon practically stood up in the little cup. But none of us were ready for it, him least of all. He still had lots to accomplish in life.'

'Like what?'

He hoped the low light would disguise the tightness of his smile. 'World domination.'

'He got halfway there, at least,' she murmured.

'WestCorp and all its holdings are just an average-sized fish on our particular reef.'

'I've seen some of those holdings; they're nothing to sneeze at.'

Rich tensed. That's right; she'd done her homework on him. He searched her gaze for a clue but found only interest. And compassion.

So Mila hadn't dug so deep that she'd found Wardoo. She wasn't skilled enough at subterfuge to have that knowledge in her head and be able to hide it. Of course it wouldn't have occurred to her to look. Why would it? And Wardoo—big as it was—was still only a small pastoral holding compared to some of WestCorp's mining and resource interests. She'd probably tired of her search long before getting to the smaller holdings at the end of the list.

'For a woman who hangs out with sea stars and coral for a living you seem to know a lot about the Western Australian corporate scene. I wouldn't have thought it would interest you.'

He saw her flush more in the sweep of her lashes on her cheeks in the moonlight than in her colour. 'Normally, no—'

Out on the water, a few gulls appeared, dipping and soaring, only to dip again at the glittering surface. The moon might not be large but it was high now.

'Oh! We're on!' Mila said, excitement bubbling in her voice.

Compared to the last time she'd stripped off in front of him, this time she did it with far less modesty. It only took a few seconds to slide the strings holding up her slip of a dress off her shoulders and step out of the pooled fabric, leaving only bare feet and white bikini. Her shell necklace followed and she piled both on the table with the same casual concern that she'd balled up the paper from their fish and chips. She gathered her snorkelling gear as Rich shed a few layers down to his board shorts and he followed her tensely to the high tide mark. Their gear on, she handed him a headlamp to match her own and a calico net.

There was something about doing this together—as partners. He trusted Mila not to put him in any kind of danger, and trusting her felt like an empowered decision. And empowerment felt a little like control.

And that was all he needed to step into the dark shallows.

'What do I do with this?' he asked, waving the net around his head, as if it was meant for butterflies.

'Just hold it a foot above any coral that's erupting. Ten seconds maximum. Then find a coral that looks totally different to the first and repeat the process.'

'This is high stakes.'

He meant that glibly but he knew by the pause as she studied him that, for her, it absolutely was.

'You can't get it wrong. Come on.'

She waded in ahead of him and his headlamp slashed across her firm, slim body as she went. Given they were on departmental business, it felt wrong to be checking out a fellow scientist. It would have helped if she'd worn a white lab coat instead of a white bikini.

Focus.

The inky water swallowed them up, and its vastness demanded his full attention even as his

mind knew it wasn't particularly deep. He fought
to keep a map of the lagoon in his head so that his
subconscious had something to reference when
it was deciding how much adrenaline to pump
through his system.

They were on the shallow side of the drop-
off, where everything was warm and golden
and filled with happy little sea creatures during the day. There was no reason that should
change just because it was dark. Robbed of one of
his key senses, his others heightened along with
his imagination. In that moment he almost understood how Mila saw the reef. The water was
silky-smooth and soft where it brushed his bare
skin. Welcoming.

Decidedly un-soupy.

He kept Mila's fins—two of them this time—
just inside the funnel of light coming from his
headlamp. Beyond the cone of both their lights
it was the inkiest of blacks. But Mila swam con-
fidently on and the sandy lagoon floor fell away
from them until the first corals started to appear
a dozen metres offshore.

'They need a good couple of metres of water
above them to do this,' she puffed, raising her

head for a moment and pushing out her snorkel mouthpiece. Her long hair glued to her neck and shoulders and her golden skin glittered wet in his lamplight. 'So that the receding tide will carry their spawn bundles away to a new site while the embryos mature. Get ready…'

He mirrored her deep breath and then submerged, kicking down to the reef's surface. At first, there was nothing. Just the odd little bit of detritus floating across his field of light, but between one fin-kick and the next he swam straight into a plume of spawning coral. Instantly, he was inside a snow dome. Hundreds of tiny bundles wafted around him on the water's current, making their way to the surface. Pink. White. Glowing in the lamplight against the endless black background of night ocean. As each one met his skin, it was like rain—or tiny reverse hailstones—plinking onto him from below then rolling off and carrying on its determined journey to the surface. As soft as a breath. Utterly surreal. All around them, tiny bait fish darted, unconcerned by their presence, and picked off single, unlucky bundles. The bigger fish kept their distance and gorged themselves just out of view and, though he knew that *even bigger* fish with much sharper teeth probably watched them from the darkness, he found it difficult to care in light of this once-in-a-lifetime moment.

Mila was right.

It was spectacular.

And he might have missed it if not for her.

He surfaced for air again, glanced at the lights of the beach car park to stay oriented and then plugged his snorkel and returned to a few metres below. Just on the edge of his lamp, Mila back-swam over a particularly active plate coral and held her net aloft, letting the little bundles just float right into its mesh embrace. He turned to the nearby staghorn and did the same. On his, the spawn came off in smoky plumes and it was hard to know which was coral and which was some local fish timing its own reproductive activity within the smokescreen of much more obvious targets. He scooped it all up regardless. For every spawn bundle he caught, thousands more were being released.

Besides, the little fish were picking off many more than he was.

Ten seconds...

A sea jelly floated across the shaft of his lamp, glowing, but it was only when a cuttlefish did the same that he stopped to wonder. He'd only ever seen them dead on the seashore—as a kid he'd used them to dig out moats on sandcastles—like small surfboards. Live and lamplit, the cuttlefish glowed with translucent beauty and busied itself chasing down a particular spawn bundle, with a dozen crazily swimming legs.

But, as he raised his eyes, the shaft of his light filled with Mila, her limbs gently waving in a way the cuttlefish could only dream of, pink-white spawn snowing in reverse all around her, her eyes behind her mask glinting and angled. He didn't need to see her smile to feel its effect on him.

She was born to be here.

And he was honoured to be allowed to visit.

The reef at night reminded him of an eighties movie he'd seen. A dying metropolis, three hundred years from now, saturated with acid rain and blazing with neon, the skies crowded with grungy air transport, the streets far below pocked with dens and cavities of danger and the under-belly that thrived there.

This reef was every bit as busy and systematic as that futuristic world. Just far more beautiful.

She surfaced for a breath near to him.

'Ready to go in?' she asked.

'Nope.' Not nearly.

She smiled. 'It's been an hour, Rich.'

He kicked his legs below the surface and re-alised how much thicker the water had become in that time. 'You're kidding?'

'Time flies...'

Yeah. It really did. He couldn't remember the last time he'd felt this relaxed. Yet energised at the same time.

'I'm happy with that haul,' she said. 'I missed the *Porites* coral last year so they'll be awesome for the spawn bank.'

'Is that what I can smell?' he said, nostrils twitching at the pungent odour.

'It's probably better not to think about exactly what we're swimming in,' she puffed, staying afloat. 'But trust me when I say it's much better being out here in freshly erupted spawn than tomorrow in day-old spawn. Or the day after.'

She deftly twisted her catch net and then his so that the contents could not escape and then they turned for shore. They had drifted out further than he'd thought but still well within the confines of the lagoon. He could only imagine what a feeding frenzy this night would be beyond the flats where the outer reef spread. In the shallow water, she passed him the nets and then kicked free of her fins to jog ashore and collect the big plastic tub waiting there. She half filled it with clear seawater and then used her snorkelling mask to pour more over the top of her reversed net, swilling out the captured spawn into their watery new home. Maskful after maskful finally got all of his in too. They wrestled the heavy container up to their table together.

After the weightlessness of an hour in the dystopian underworld his legs felt like clumsy, useless trunks and he longed for the ease and effectiveness and freedom of his fins.

Freedom...

'So what did you think?' Mila asked, straightening.

Because they'd carried the tub together, she was standing much closer to him than she ever had before and her head came to just below his shoulder, forcing her to peer up at him with clear green eyes. Even bedraggled and wet, and with red pressure marks from her mask around her face, he wasn't sure he'd ever seen anything quite as beautiful. Except maybe the electric snowfield of spawning coral rising all around her as she did her best mermaid impersonation.

He'd never wanted to kiss someone so much in his life.

'Speechless,' he murmured instead. 'It was everything you said it would be.'

'Now do you get it?'

Somehow he knew what she was really asking. *Now do you get* me?

He raised a hand and brushed her cheek with his knuckles, tucking a strand of soggy hair behind her ear. She sucked in a breath and leaned, almost easily, into his touch. It was the first time she hadn't flinched away from him.

His chest tightened even as it felt as if it had expanded two-fold with the pride of that.

'Yeah,' he breathed. 'I think I do. What is it like for you?'

'A symphony. So many sounds all working together.' Her eyes glittered at the memory. 'Not necessarily in harmony—just a wash of sound. The coral bundles are like tiny percussions and they build and they build as the sea fills with them and the ones that touch my skin are like—' she searched around her as if the word she needed was hovering nearby '—a mini firework. Hundreds of tiny explosions. The coral itself is so vibrant under light it just sings to me. Seduces. Breathtaking, except that I'm already holding my breath.' She dropped her head and her wet locks swayed. 'I can't explain it.'

He brought her gaze back up with a finger beneath her chin. His other hand came up to frame her cheek. 'I think I envy you your superpower right now.'

Lips the same gentle pink as the coral spawn parted slightly and mesmerised his gaze just as the little bundles had.

'It has its moments,' she breathed.

Mila was as much a product of this reef as anything he saw out there. Half-mermaid and easily as at home in the water as she was on land. Born of the Saltwater People and she would die in it, living it, loving it.

Protecting it.

This land was technically his heritage too, yet he had no such connection with it and no such protective instincts. He'd been raised to work it and maximise its yield. To exploit it.

For the first time ever he doubted the philosophy he'd been raised with. And he doubted himself.

Was he exploiting Mila too? Mining her for her knowledge and expertise? Wouldn't kissing her when she didn't know the truth about him just be another kind of exploitation? As badly as he wanted to lower his mouth onto hers, until he rectified *that*, any kiss he stole would be just that...

Stolen.

'You have spawn in your hair,' he murmured as she peered up at him.

It said something about how used to the distance of others Mila was that she was so unsurprised when he stepped back.

'I'm sure that's the least of it,' she said. 'Let's

get this all back to my place and we can both clean up.'

He retreated a step, then another, and he lifted the heavy spawn-rich container to save Mila the chore. Her dress snagged on her damp skin as she wriggled back into it but then she gathered up the rest of their gear and followed him up to her truck.

CHAPTER SEVEN

IT ONLY OCCURRED to Mila as she pulled up out the front that Rich was the first person she'd ever brought into this place. When she needed to liaise with work people she usually drove the long road north to the department's branch office or met them at some beach site somewhere. She never came with them here, to the little stack of converted transport modules that served as both home and office.

Safe, private spaces.

Rich stood by her four-wheel drive, looking at the two-storey collection of steel.

'Are those…shipping containers?'

The back of her mouth filled with something between fried chicken and old leather. She looked at the corrugated steel walls in their mismatched, faded primary colours as he might see them and definitely found them wanting.

'Up here the regular accommodation is saved

for the tourists,' she said. 'Behind the scenes, everyone lives in pretty functional dwellings. But we make them homey inside. Come on in.'

She led him around the back of the efficient dwelling where a weathered timber deck stretched out between the 'U' of sea containers on three sides—double-storey in the centre and single-storey adjoining on the left and right. He stumbled to a halt at the sight of her daybed—an old timber dinghy, tipped on an angle and filled with fat, inviting cushions. A curl of old canvas hung above it between the containers like a crashing wave. He stood, speechless, and stared at her handiwork.

'You're going to see a bit of upcycling in the next quarter-hour…' she warned, past the sour milk of self-consciousness.

Mila pushed open the double doors on the sea container to her left and stepped into her office. Despite the unpromising exterior, inside, it looked much like any other workspace except that her furniture was a bit more eclectic than the big city corporate office Rich was probably used to. A weathered old beach shack door for a desk, with a pair of deep filing cabinets for legs. An old paint-streaked ladder mounted lengthways on the wall served as bookshelves for her biology textbooks and her work files. The plain walls were decorated with a panoramic photograph she had taken of her favourite lagoon, enlarged and mounted in three parts behind mismatched window frames salvaged from old fishing shacks from down the coast.

Rich stared at the artwork.

'My view when I'm working,' she puffed, fighting the heat of a blush. 'Could you put that by the door?'

He positioned the opaque tub by the glass doors so that the moonlight could continue to work its magic on the coral spawn within until she could freeze them in the morning. Those first few hours of moonlight seemed critical to a good fertilisation result; why else had nature designed them to bob immediately to the surface instead of sink to the seafloor?

She killed the light and turned to cross the deck. 'I inherited this stack from someone else when I first moved out of home, but it was pretty functional then. I like to think I've improved it.'

She opened French windows immediately opposite her office and led Rich inside. His eyes had barely managed to stop bulging at her makeshift office before they were goggling again.

'You did all this?' he asked, looking around.

Her furniture mostly consisted of another timber sailing boat cut into parts and sanded within an inch of its life before being waxed until it was glossy. The stern half stood on its fat end at the end of the room and acted as a bookshelf and display cabinet, thanks to some handiwork flipping the boat's seats into shelves; its round little middle sat upturned at the centre of the space and held the glass that made it a coffee table, and its pointed bow was wall-mounted and served as a side table.

'I had some help from one of Coral Bay's old sea dogs, but otherwise, yes, I made most of this. I hate to see anything wasted. Feel free to look around.'

She jogged up polished timber steps to the bedroom that sat on top of the centremost sea container—the one that acted as kitchen, bathroom and laundry. She rustled up some dry clothes and an armful of towels and then padded back down to take a quick shower. Rich hadn't moved his feet but he'd twisted a little, presumably to peer around him. Was it in disbelief? In surprise?

In horror?

To her, it was personalised expression—her little haven filled with things that brought her pleasure. But what did Rich see? Did he view it as the junkyard pickings of some kind of hoarder?

His eyes were fixed overhead, on the lighting centrepiece of the room. A string of bud lights twisted and wove back on itself but each tiny bulb was carefully mounted inside a sea urchin she'd found on the shore outside of the sanctuary zone. Some big. Some small. All glowing their own delicate shades of pinks and orange. The whole thing tangled around an artful piece of driftwood she'd just loved.

The room filled with sour milk again and it killed her that she could feel so self-conscious about something that had brought her so much joy to create. And still did. She refused to defend it even though she burned to.

'I'll be just five minutes,' she announced, tossing the towel over her shoulder. 'Then you can clean up too.'

She scurried through the kitchen to the bathroom at the back of the sea container. If you didn't know what you were standing in you might think you were in some kind of upmarket beach shack, albeit eclectically furnished. Rich had five minutes to look his fill at all her weird stuff and then he'd be in here—her eyes drifted up to the white, round lightshade to which she'd attached streaming lengths of plaited fishing net until the whole thing resembled a cheerful bathroom jellyfish—for better or worse.

When she emerged, rinsed and clean-haired, Rich was studying up close the engineering on a tiered wall unit made of pale driftwood. She moved up next to him and lit the tea lights happily sitting on its shelves. They cast a gentle glow over that side of the room.

'Will I find an ordinary light fitting anywhere in your house?' he murmured down at her.

She had to think about it. 'The lamp in the office is pretty regular.' If you didn't count the tiny sea stars glued to its stand. 'This is one of my favourites.'

She lit another tea light sitting all alone on the boat bow side table except for a tiny piece of beach detritus that sat with it. It looked like nothing more than a minuscule bit of twisted seaweed. But, as the flame caught behind it, a shadow cast on the nearby wall and Rich was drawn by the flickering shape that grew as the flame did.

'I found the poor, dried seahorse on the marina shore when it was first built,' she said. 'Took me ages to think how I could celebrate it.'

He turned and just stared, something rather like confusion in his blue gaze.

Mila handed him a small stack of guest towels and pointed him in the direction of the bathroom. 'Take your time.'

As soon as he was safely out of view, she sagged against the kitchen bench. Nothing should have upstaged the fact that there was a naked man showering just ten feet away in her compact little bathroom, but Rich had given her spectacular fodder for distraction.

That kiss...

Not an actual kiss, but nearly. Cheek-brushing and chest-heaving and lingering looks. Enough that she'd been throbbing candyfloss while her pulse had tumbled over itself like a crashing wave. Lucky she'd built up such excellent lung capacity because she'd flat-out forgotten to breathe during the whole experience. Anyone else might have passed out.

'An almost-kiss isn't an actual kiss,' she lectured herself under her breath.

Even if it was the closest she'd come in a long, long time. Rich had been overwhelmed by his experience on the reef and had reached out instinctively, but—really—who wanted to kiss a woman soaked in spawn?

'No one.'

She rustled up a second mug and put the kettle on to boil. It took about the same time to bubble as the ninety seconds Rich did to shower and change back into his black sweater and jeans. When he emerged from the door next to her, all pink and freshly groomed, the bathroom's steam mingled with the kettle's.

'I made you tea,' she murmured.

He smiled as he took the mug. 'It's been a long time since I've had tea.'

Her eyes immediately hunted for coffee. 'You don't like it?'

'It's just that coffee's more a thing in the corporate world. I've fallen out of practice. It was a standard at boarding school until eleventh form, when we were allowed to upgrade to a harder core breakfast beverage.'

She started rummaging in the kitchen. 'I have some somewhere…'

He met her eyes and held them. 'I would like to drink tea with you, Mila.'

She couldn't look away; she could barely breathe a reply. 'Okay.'

He looked around her humble home again. 'I really like your place.'

'It's different to the *Portus*.'

He laughed. 'It's not a boat, for one thing. But it suits you. It's unique.'

Unique. Yep, that was one word for her.

'I hate to see anything wasted,' she said again. Her eyes went to her sea urchin extravaganza. 'And I hate to see beautiful things die. This is a way I can keep them alive and bring the reef inside at the same time.'

He studied her light art as if it was by a Renaissance sculptor, his brows drawn, deep in thought.

'What is your home like?' she went on when he didn't reply.

The direct question brought his gaze back to

her. 'It's not a *home*, for a start. I don't feel like I've had one of those since... A long time.' He peered around again. 'But it's nothing like this.'

No. She couldn't imagine him surrounded by anything other than quality. She sank ahead of him onto one of two sofas made out of old travelling chests. The sort that might have washed up after a shipwreck. The sort that was perfect to have upholstered into insanely comfortable seats.

Rich frowned a little as he examined the seat's engineering.

'Home is something you come back to, isn't it?' he went on. 'About the only thing I have that meets that definition is the *Portus*. I feel different when I step aboard. Changed. Maybe she's my home.'

Mila sipped at her tea in the silence that followed and watched Rich grow less and less comfortable in her company.

'Is everything all right, Rich?' she finally braved.

He glanced up at her and then sighed. Long and deep.

'Mila, there's something I haven't told you.'

The cloves made a brief reappearance but she

pushed through the discomfort. Trust came more easily with every minute she spent in Rich's company.

'Keeping secrets, Mr Grundy?' she quipped.

'That's just it,' he went on, ignoring her attempt at humour. 'I'm not Mr Grundy. At least...I am, and I'm not.'

She pressed back into the soft upholstery and gave him her full attention.

He lifted bleak eyes. 'Nancy Dawson married a Grundy.'

Awareness flooded in on a wave of nostalgia. 'Oh, that's right. Jack. I forgot because everyone up here knows them as Dawson. Wait...are you a relative of Jack Grundy? Ten times removed?'

'No times removed, actually.' Rich took a long sip of his tea. As if it were his last. 'Jack was my great-grandfather.'

Mila just stared. 'But that means...'

Nancy's Point. She'd stood there and lectured him about his own great-grandmother. The more immediate ramification took a little longer to sink in. She sat upright and placed her still steaming mug onto the little midships coffee table. The only way to disguise the sudden tremble of her fingers was to lay them flat on the thighs of her yoga pants. Unconsciously bracing herself.

'Are you a Dawson? Of the Wardoo Dawsons?'

Rich took a deep breath. 'I'm *the* Dawson. The only son of an only son. I hold the pastoral rights on Wardoo Station and the ten thousand square kilometres around it.'

Mila's hands dug deeper into her thighs. 'But that means...'

'It means I hold the lease on the land that Coral Bay sits on.'

The back of her throat stung with the taste of nail varnish and it was all she could do to whisper, 'You own my town?'

Rich straightened. 'The only thing I *own* is the Station infrastructure. But the lease is what has the value. And I hold that, presently.'

Her brain finally caught up and the nail varnish dissipated. 'Wardoo is yours.'

Because there was no Wardoo without the Dawsons. Just as there was no Coral Bay without them either.

Rich took a deep breath before answering. 'It is.'

Her eyes came up. 'Then you've been stop-

ping the developers in their tracks! I thought
you were one!'

His skin greyed off just a bit. Maybe he wasn't
comfortable with overt gushing, but the strong
mango of gratitude made it impossible for her
to stop.

'WestCorp has been denying access for third-
party development, yes—'

Whatever that little bit of careful corporate
speak meant. All she heard was that *Rich* was
the reason there were no towering hotels on her
reef. *Rich* had kept everyone but the state government out of the lands bordering the World
Heritage Marine Park. *Rich* was her corporate
guardian angel.

Despite herself, despite everything she knew
about people and every screaming sense she
knew she'd be triggering, Mila tipped herself forward and threw her arms wide around his broad
shoulders.

'Thank you,' she gushed, pressing herself into
the hug. 'Thank you for my reef.'

CHAPTER EIGHT

RICH COULDN'T REMEMBER a time that he'd been more comfortable in someone's arms yet so excruciatingly uncomfortable as well.

Mila had only grasped half the truth.

Because he had only told half of it.

He let his own hands slide up and contribute to Mila's fervent embrace, but it was brief and it took little physical effort to curl his fingers and ease her slightly back from him. The emotional effort was much higher; she was warm and soft under his hands and she felt incredibly right there—speaking of going *home*—yet he felt more of a louse than when he'd nearly kissed her earlier.

Telling her had been the right thing to do but, in his head, this moment was going to go very differently. He'd steeled himself for her shock, her disappointment. Maybe for an escaped tear or two that he'd been keeping the truth from her. Instead, he got...this.

Gratitude.

He'd confessed his identity now but Mila only saw half the picture... The half that made him a hero, looking out for the underdog and the underdog's reef. She had no sense for the politics and game playing behind every access refusal. The prioritising.

It wasn't noble... It was corporate strategy.

'Don't be too quick to canonise me, Mila,' he murmured as she withdrew from the spontaneous hug, blushing. The gentle flush matched the colour she'd been when she came out of the bathroom. 'It's business. It's not personal. I hadn't even seen the reef until you showed me.'

Even now he was avoiding putting the puzzle fully together for her. It would only take a few words to confess that—yeah, he was still a developer and he was planning on developing her reef. But he wasn't strong enough to do that while he was still warm from her embrace.

'How could you go to Wardoo and not visit such a famous coast?' she asked.

'Actually, I've never been to Wardoo either,' he confessed further. 'I flew over it once, years ago.'

The quizzical smile turned into a gape. 'What? Why?'

'Because there's no need. I get reports and updates from the caretaking team. To me, it's just a remote business holding at the end of one of my spreadsheets.'

The words on his lips made him tense. As though the truth wasn't actually the truth.

Her gape was now a stare. 'No. Really?'

'Really.' He shrugged.

'But… It's *Wardoo*. It's your home.'

'I never grew up there, Mila. It holds no meaning for me.'

A momentary flash of his eight-year-old self tumbled beneath his determination for it to *be* the truth.

She scrabbled upright again and perched on her seat, leaning towards him. 'You need to go, Rich.'

No. He really didn't.

'You need to go and see it in its context, not in some photograph. Smell it and taste it and…'

'Taste it?'

'Okay, maybe that's just me, but won't you at

least visit the people who run it for you? Let them show you their work?'

It was his turn to frown. Her previous jibe about *minions* hit home again.

'I'm sure they'd be delighted with a short-notice visit from their CEO,' he drawled.

She considered him. 'You won't know if you don't ask.'

He narrowed his eyes. 'You're very keen for me to visit, Mila. What am I missing?'

Her expression grew suspiciously innocent. 'I *might* be thinking about the fact that you don't have a car. And that I do—'

'And you're offering to lend it to me?' he shot back, his face just as impassive. 'Thanks, that's kind of you.'

Which made it sound as if he was considering going. When had that happened?

'Actually, it's kind of hinky to drive. I'd better take you. Road safety and all.'

'You don't know the roads. You've never been out there.'

Hoisted by her own petard.

'Okay, fine. Then take me in return for the

coral spawn.' She shuffled forward. 'I would give anything to see Wardoo.'

Glad one of them was so keen. 'You know there's no reef out there, right? Just scrub and dirt.'

'Come on, Rich, it's a win-win—I get to see Wardoo and you get to have a reason to go there.'

'I don't need a reason to go there.'

And he didn't particularly *want* to. Though he did, very much, want to see the excited colour in Mila's cheeks a little bit longer. It reminded him of the flush as he'd stroked her cheek. And it did make a kind of sense to check it out since he was up here on an official fact-finding mission. After all, how convincing was he going to be if that government bureaucrat discovered he'd never actually been to the property? Photos and monthly reports could only do so much.

'What time?' he sighed.

Mila's eyes glittered like the emeralds they were, triumphant. 'I have a quickish task to do at low tide, but it's on the way to Wardoo so... Eight?'

'Does this *task* involve anything else slimy, soupy or slippery?' he worried.

'Maybe.' She laughed. 'It involves the reef.'

Of course it did.

'How wet will I be getting?'

'You? Not at all. I might, depending on the tide.'

'Okay then.' He could happily endure one last opportunity to see Mila in her natural habitat. Before he told her the full truth. And he could give her the gift of Wardoo, before pulling the happy dream they were both living out from under her too.

The least he could do, maybe.

'Eight it is, then.'

Her gaze glowed her pleasure and Rich just let himself swim there for a few moments. Below it all, he knew he was only delaying the inevitable, but there really was nothing to gain by telling her now instead of tomorrow.

'I should get back to the *Portus*,' he announced, reaching into his pocket for his phone. 'Need my beauty sleep if I'm going to wow the minions to-morrow.'

Her perfect skin flushed again as she remem-bered her own words and who she'd been talking about all along. But she handled the embarrassment as she handled everything—graciously. She crossed the small room to get her keys off their little hook.

'I'll drive you to the marina.'

Not surprisingly, given the marina was only a few minutes away, there was no sign of Damo when they climbed out of the four-wheel drive at the deserted ramp, although Mila could clearly see the *Portus* waiting out beyond the reef. Had it done laps out there the whole night, like a pacing attendant waiting for its master?

'He won't be long,' Rich murmured as a floodlight made its way steadily across the darkness that was the sea beyond the reef. The speed limits still applied even though no one else was using the channel. They weren't there to protect the boats.

'Did you enjoy dinner?' Rich asked after a longish, silence-filled pause. He turned closer to her in the darkness.

She'd totally forgotten the eating part of the evening. All she'd been fixating on was the looking part, the touching part. The just-out-of-the-shower part.

'Very much,' she said, looking up to him. 'Always happy not to go into a crowded building.'

'Thank you for letting me tag along on the spawn; it really was very beautiful.'

It was impossible not to chuckle but—this close and in this much darkness—it came out sounding way throatier than she meant it. 'I'm pretty sure I bullied you into coming.'

Just like she'd talked her way into Wardoo tomorrow.

'Happy to have been bullied then. I never could have imagined...'

No. It really was *un*imaginable until you'd seen it. She liked knowing that they had that experience in common now. Every shared experience they had brought them that little bit closer. And now that she knew he was a Dawson...every experience would help to secure the borders against developers even more.

A stiff breeze kicked up off the water and reminded Mila that she was still in the light T-shirt and yoga pants she'd shrugged into in her steamy little bathroom inside her warm little house. Gooseflesh prickled, accompanied by imaginary wings fluttering as the bumps raced up her skin.

'You should head home,' Rich immediately said as she rubbed her arms. 'It's cold.'

'No—'

She didn't want to leave. She didn't want to wait until eight a.m. to see him again. She wasn't ready to leave this man who turned out to have had the back of everything she cared about for all these years. If he asked her back to his boat to spend the night she was ready to say yes.

'I'm good.'

Large hands found her upper arms in the light from the silvered moon and added their warmth to her cold skin. Harps immediately joined the fluttering wings.

'Here...'

Rich moved around close behind her and then rubbed his hands up and down her arms, bringing her back against his hard, warm, sweater-clad chest. He'd shifted from a client to an acquaintance somewhere around the visit to Yardi Creek, and from acquaintance to a friend when she'd agreed to have dinner. But exactly when did they become *arm-rubbing* kinds of friends? Was it when they'd stood so close by the shore this evening? When they'd shared the majesty of the spawn event? The not-quite kiss?

Did it even matter? The multiple sensations of his hands on hers, his body against hers was a kind of heaven she'd secretly believed she would never experience.

It was only when she saw the slash of the tender's arriving floodlight on the back of her eyelids that she realised they'd fluttered shut.

Rich stepped away and the harps faded to nothing at the loss of his skin on hers.

'I'll see you here at eight,' he said, far more composed than she felt. But then his big frame blocked the moonlight as he bent to kiss her cheek. His words were a hot caress against her ear and the gooseflesh worsened.

'Sleep well.'

Pfff... As if.

Before she could reply, he had stepped away and she mourned not only the warmth of his hands but now the gentle brush of his lips too. Too, too brief. He stepped down onto the varnished pier out to the tender and left her. Standing here, watching him walk away from her, those narrow jeans-clad hips swinging even in the dim moonlight, was a little too much like self-harm and so she turned to face her truck and took the few steps she needed to cross back to it.

At the last moment she heard a crunch that wasn't her own feet on the crushed gravel marina substrate.

'Mila...'

She pivoted into Rich's return and he didn't even pause as he walked hard up against her and bent again, to her lips this time. His kiss was soft but it lingered. It explored. It blew her little mind. And it came with a sensation overload. He took her too much by surprise to invoke the citrus of anticipation but it kicked in now and mingled with the strong, candy surge of attraction as a tiny corner of her mind wondered breathlessly how long his kiss could last. Waves crashed and she knew it wasn't on the nearby shore; it was what kissing gave her, though not always like this... Not always accompanied by skin harps and the crackle of fireplace that was the heat of Rich's mouth on her own. And all that oak moss...

Her head spun with want as much as the breathless surprise of Rich's stealthy return.

'I should have done that hours ago,' he murmured at last, breathing fast. 'I wanted to right after the coral.'

'Why didn't you?' Belatedly, she realised she was probably supposed to protest his presumption, or say something witty, or be grown up and blasé about it. But really, all she wanted to know was why they hadn't been kissing all evening.

'I wanted you to know about me. Who I was. So you had the choice.'

Oh, kissing him was a *choice*? That was a laugh, and not because he'd sneaked up on her and made the first move. She'd been thinking about his mouth for days now.

There was no choice.

But she was grateful for the consideration.

'I like who you are,' she murmured. 'Thank you for telling me.'

Besides, she was the last person who could judge anyone else for keeping themselves private.

He dipped his head again and sent the harps a-harping and the fire a-crackling for more precious moments. Then he straightened and stepped back.

'Tomorrow then,' he said and he and his conflicted gaze were gone, jogging down the pier towards the *Portus'* waiting tender.

Mila sagged against her open car door and watched until he was out of sight. Even then, she stared at the inky ocean and imagined the small boat making its way until it reappeared as a shadow against the well-lit *Portus*. Impossible to see Rich climb aboard at this distance but she imagined that too; in her mind's eye she saw him slumping down on that expansive sofa amid the polished chrome and glass. She tried to imagine him checking his phone or picking up a book or even stretching out on that king-sized bed and watching the night sky through the wraparound windows, but it was easier to imagine him settling in behind his laptop at the workstation and getting a few more hours of corporate in before his head hit any kind of pillow.

That was just who he was. And it was where he came from.

A whale shark couldn't change its spots.

Except this one—just maybe—could.

CHAPTER NINE

MILA TOOK A careful knife to the reef and carved out a single oyster from a crowded corner, working carefully not to injure or loosen the rest. Then she did it again at another stack. And again. And again. On the way out to this remote bay, she'd told Rich that her department's licence called for five test oysters every month and a couple of simple observational tests to monitor oyster condition and keep them free of the disease that was ravaging populations down the east coast of the country.

Rich held the little bag for her as she dropped them in one by one.

She smiled shy thanks, though not quite at him. 'For a CEO you make an excellent apprentice ranger.'

So far this morning the two of them had been doing a terrific job of ignoring exactly what it was that had gone down between them last night. The kissing part, not the sharing of secrets part. One was planned, the other... Not so much. He hadn't even known he was going to do it until he'd felt his feet twisting on the pier and striding back towards her.

'Now I understand your fashion choice,' he murmured, nodding at her high-vis vest emblazoned with the department logo. It wasn't the most flattering thing he'd seen her in since they'd met yet she still managed to make it seem...intriguing.

'Don't want anyone thinking they can just help themselves to oysters here,' she said. 'This is inside the sanctuary zone.'

Not that there was a soul around yet. The tide was way too low to be of interest to snorkelers and the fishermen had too much respect for their equipment to try tossing a line in at this razor-ridden place.

They waded ashore and Mila laid the five knotted shells out on the tailgate of her four-wheel drive. She placed a dog-eared laminated number above each, photographed it and then set about her testing. All that busyness was a fantastic way of not needing to make eye contact with him.

Was she embarrassed? Did she regret participating quite so enthusiastically in last night's experimental kiss? Or was she just as focused on her work as he could be when he was in the zone? Given how distracted he'd been last night, going over and over the proposal, it was hard to imagine ever being in the zone again.

Mila picked one oyster up and gently knocked its semi-open shell. It closed immediately but with no great urgency.

'That's a four,' she told him, and he dutifully wrote it down on the form she'd given him.

The others were all fours too, and one super-speedy five. That made her happy. She'd clearly opened an oyster or three in her time and she made quick work of separating each one from its top shell by a swift knife move to its hinge. She wafted the inner scent of each towards her nostrils before dipping her finger in and then placing it in her mouth to taste its juices. He wrote down her observations as she voiced them.

'If these five exemplars are responsive, fresh

and the flesh is opaque then it's a good sign of the health of the whole oyster community,' she said.

'What do you do with them, then—toss them back?'

'These five are ambassadors for their kind. I usually wedge the shells back in to become part of the stack, but I don't waste the meat.'

'And by that you mean...?'

'I eat them,' she said with a grin. 'Want to help?'

Rich frowned. 'Depends on whether you have any red wine vinegar on hand.'

She used the little knife to shuck the first of them and flip it to study its underside. Then she held up the oyster sample in front of her lips like a salute. *'Au naturel.'*

Down it went. She repeated the neat move and handed the finished shuck to him.

His eyebrows raised as soon as he bit down on the ultra-fresh mollusc. 'Melon!'

'Yeah, kind of. Salty melon.'

'Even to you?'

She smiled. 'Even to me. With a bonus hit of *astute.*'

Rich couldn't really see how a hibernating lump

of muscle could have any personality at all but he was prepared to go with 'astute'. He'd never managed to taste the 'ambition' in vintage wine either, but he was prepared to believe that connoisseurs at the fancy restaurants he frequented could.

Maybe Mila was just a nature connoisseur.

Oyster number three and four went the same way and then there was only the one left. He offered it to Mila. 'You know what they say about oysters…'

She blinked at him. 'Excellent for your immune system and bone strength?'

He stared at her, trying to gauge whether she was serious. He loved not being able to read her. How long had it been since someone surprised him?

'Yeah, that's what they say.'

It was only when she smiled, slow and sexy, that he knew *she* knew. But obviously she wasn't about to mention it in light of last night's illicit kiss.

She gasped, scribbling in her log what she'd found on the oyster's underside. 'A pearl.'

Rich peered at the small cream mass. It wasn't

much of one but it undoubtedly *was* a pearl. 'Is that a good sign?'

'Not really.' Mila poked at it carefully. 'It could have formed in response to a parasite. Too much of that would be a bad sign for these stacks.'

'Pearls are a defect?' he asked.

'"Out of a flaw comes beauty",' Mila quoted.

She might as well have been describing herself.

She lifted it out with her blade and rinsed it in the seawater, then swallowed the last of the oyster flesh.

'Here,' she said, handing it to him. 'A souvenir.'

'Because you have so many littering your house?'

Just how many had she found in her time?

'It's reasonably rare to find a wild one,' she said, still smiling. 'This is only my second in all the time I've been working here. But I don't feel right about keeping them; I'm lucky enough just to do this for a living without profiting from it further. I gave the last one away to a woman with three noisy kids.'

Rich stared. She was like a whole different species to him. 'Do you know what they're worth?'

'Not so much when they're this small and malformed, I don't think.' She laid it out on her hand and let the little lump flip over on her wet palm. 'But I prefer them like this. Rough and nature-formed. Though it's weird, I don't get any kind of personality off them. I wonder why.'

She studied it a moment longer, as if *willing* it to perform for her.

'Here...' She finally thrust her hand out. 'Something to remember Coral Bay by. Sorry it's not bigger.'

Something deep in his chest protested. Did she imagine he cared about that? When he looked at the small, imperfect pearl he would remember the small, imperfect woman who had given it to him.

And how perfect her imperfections made her.

He closed his hand around the lumpy gem. 'Thank you.'

She took the empty shell parts and jogged back into the water to wedge them back into the stacks as foundation for future generations, then she returned and packed up. Rich took the opportunity to watch her move, and work, without making her self-conscious.

He found he quite liked to just watch her.

'Okay,' she finally puffed. 'All done for the

month. Shall we get going? Did you tell Wardoo you were coming?'

'Panic duly instigated, yes.'

She smiled at him and he wondered when he'd started counting the minutes between them. She'd smiled more at him in the last hour than she had in the entire time he'd known her. It was uncomfortably hard not to connect it to her misapprehension that he was some kind of crusading, conservation good guy.

'I think you'll like it. This country really is very beautiful in its own unique way.'

As he followed her up the path to her car all he could think about was an old phrase...

Takes one to know one.

Their arrival at Wardoo was decidedly low-key. If not for the furtive glance of a man crossing between one corrugated outbuilding and the next she'd have thought no one was all that interested in Rich's arrival. But that sideways look spoke volumes. It was more the kind of surreptitious play-down-the-moment peek reserved for politicians or rock stars.

Or royalty.

Some of the men who had worked Wardoo their whole adult lives might never have seen a Dawson in person. *Grundy*, she reminded herself.

A wide grin in a weathered, masculine face met them, introduced himself as the Station foreman and offered to show them, first, through the homestead.

'Jared Kipling,' he said, shaking Rich's hand. 'Kip.'

She wasn't offended that Kip had forgotten to shake her hand in the fluster of meeting his long-absent boss. It saved her the anxiety of another first-time touch.

It was only when she watched Rich's body language as he stepped up onto the veranda running the full perimeter of the homestead that she realised he'd slipped back into business mode. She recognised it from that first day at Nancy's Point. Exactly when he'd stopped being quite so…corporate she wasn't as sure.

'It's vacant?' Mila asked as she stepped into the dust-free hall of Wardoo homestead ahead of the men. Despite being furnished, there was something empty about it, and not just because the polished floorboards exuded isolation the way jarrah always did for her.

Wardoo was…hollow. And somehow lifeless.

How incredibly sad. Not what she had imagined at all.

'Most of our crew live in transportables on site or in town. We keep the house for the Dawsons,' Kip said. 'Just in case.'

The Dawsons who had never visited? The hollowness only increased and she glanced at Rich. He kept his gaze firmly averted.

She left the men to their discussions and explored the homestead. Every room was just as clean and just as empty as the one before it. She ran her fingertips along the rich old surfaces and enjoyed the myriad sensations that came with them. When she made her way back to the living room, Rich and the foreman were deep in discussion on the unused sofas. She heard the word 'lease' before Rich shot to his feet and brought the conversation to a rapid halt.

'If you've seen enough—' Kip floundered at the sudden end to their conversation '—I can show you the operations yards and then the chopper's standing by for an aerial tour.'

Rich looked decidedly awkward too. What a novelty—to be the least socially clumsy person in a room.

'You have your own chopper?' Mila asked him, to ease the tension.

It did the trick. He gifted her a small smile that only served to remind her how many minutes it had been since the last one.

Because apparently she counted, now.

He turned for the door as if she'd been the one keeping him waiting. 'It seems I do.'

'It's a stock mustering chopper,' Kip went on, tailing them. 'There's only room for two. But it's the only way to get out to the perimeter of Wardoo and back in a day.'

'The perimeter can wait,' Rich declared. 'Just show us the highlights within striking distance by road.'

Us. As if she were some kind of permanent part of the Richard Grundy show.

She trotted along behind Rich as he toured the equipment and sheds closest to the Homestead. Of course, on a property of this scale 'close' was relative. Then they piled into a late model Land Cruiser and set off in a plume of red-brown dust to the north. Mila lost herself in the Australian scrub and let time flow over her like water as Rich and Kip discussed the operations of the cattle station. She was yet to actually see a cow.

'The herds like to range inland this time of year,' Kip said when she asked. 'While the eastern dams are full. We'll see some soon.'

She lost track of time again until the brush of knuckles on her cheek tingled her out of a light doze.

'Lunchtime,' Rich murmured.

'How long have…?' Lord, how embarrassing.

'Sorry, there was a lot of shop-talk.'

And she'd only slept fitfully last night. Something to do with being kissed half to death at the marina had left her tossing and turning and, clearly, in need of some decent sleep. Mila scurried to climb out of the comfortable vehicle ahead of him.

'The missus made you this,' Kip said, passing Rich a hamper. 'She wasn't expecting two of you but she's probably over-catered so you should be right. Follow the track down that way and you'll come to Jack's Vent. A nice spot to eat,' he told them and then raised Rich's eyebrows by adding, 'No crocs.'

'No crocs...' Rich murmured as they set off. 'Good to know.'

His twisted smile did the same to her insides, and she'd grown to relish the pineapple smell when he gave her that particular wry grin. Pineapple—just when she thought she'd had every fruit known to man.

They walked in silence as the track descended and the land around them transformed in a way that spoke of regular water. Less scrub, more trees. Less brown, more colours peppering the green vegetation. Even the surface of the dark water was freckled with oversized lily pads, some flowering with vibrant colour. Out of cracks in the rock, tall reeds grew.

They reached the edge of Jack's Vent and peered down from the rocky ledge.

Mila glanced around. 'A waterhole seems out of place here where it's so dry.'

Though it certainly was a tranquil and beautiful surprise.

'I've seen this on a map,' Rich murmured. 'It's a sinkhole, not a waterhole. A groundwater vent.'

Golden granite ringed the hole except for a narrow stock trail on the far side where Wardoo's cattle came to drink their fill of the icy, fresh, presumably artesian water, and a flatter patch of rock to their right. It looked like a natural diving platform.

'Wish I'd brought my snorkelling gear,' she murmured. 'I would love to have a look deeper in the vent.'

'You're off the clock, remember?'

'I could do that while you and Kip talk business.'

He gave her his hand to step down onto the rocky platform, which sloped right down to the water's edge. She moved right down to it and kicked off her shoes.

'It's freezing!' she squealed, dipping a toe in. 'Gorgeous.'

Rich lowered the hamper and toed off his own boots, then rolled his jeans up to his knees and followed her down to a sitting position. He gingerly sank his feet.

'There must be twenty sandwiches in here,' Mila said, looking through the hamper's contents and passing him a chilled bottle of water to match her own. 'All different.'

'I guess they were covering all bases.'

'Eager to impress, I suppose. This is a big moment for them.'

Rich snorted then turned his gaze out to the water. They ate in companionable silence but Mila felt Rich's focus drift further and further from her like the lily pads floating on the sinkhole's surface.

'For someone sitting in such a beautiful spot, you look pretty unhappy to be here,' she said when his frown grew too great. Guilt swilled around her like the water at her feet; she had nagged him to bring her. To come at all.

'Sorry,' he said, snapping his focus back to the present. 'Memories.'

She kept her frown light. 'But you haven't been here before.'

'No.' And that was all he gave her. His next words tipped the conversation back her way. 'You were the one panting to come today. How's it living up to your expectations?'

She looked around them. 'It's hard to sit somewhere like this and find fault. Wardoo offers the best of both worlds—the richness of the land and the beauty of the coast. I feel very—'

What? What was the quality she felt?

'*Comfortable* here,' she said at last. 'Maybe it's some kind of genetic memory doing its thing. Oh!'

He glanced around to see what had caught her eye.

'I just realised that both our ancestors could have sat right on this spot, separated by centuries. And now here we are again. Maybe that's why I feel so connected to you.'

Those words slipped out before she thought of the wisdom of them.

Eyes the colour of the sky blazed into her. 'Do you? Feel connected?'

Sour milk wafted around them but Rich's nostrils didn't twitch the way hers wanted to. 'You don't?'

He considered her, long and hard. 'It's futile but… I do, yes.'

Her breath tightened in a way that made her wonder whether her sandwich was refusing to go down.

'Futile?' she half breathed.

'We have such different goals.' His eyes dropped away. 'You're Saltwater People and I'm…glass-and-chrome people.'

She'd never been more grateful to not fit any particular label. That way anything felt possible.

'That's just geography, though. It doesn't change who we are at heart.'

'Doesn't it? I don't know anyone like you back home. So connected to the land…earth spirit and mermaid all at once. That's nurture, not nature. You're as much a product of this environment as those waterlilies. You wouldn't last five minutes in the city, synaesthesia or not.'

Did he have so little faith in her? 'You think I wouldn't adapt?'

'I think you'd *wither*, Mila. I think being away from this place would strip the best of you away. Just like staying here would kill me.'

'You don't like the Bay?'

Why did that thought hurt so very much?

'I like it very much but my world isn't here. I don't know how long I would be entertained by all the pretty. Not when there's work to be done.'

Did he count her in with that flippant description? She had no right to expect otherwise, yet she was undeniably tasting the leather of disappointment in the back of her throat.

'Is that what I've been doing? Entertaining you?'

The obvious answer was yes, because she was paid to show him the best of the Marine Park, but they both knew what she was really asking.

'Mila, that was—' He glanced away and back so quickly she couldn't begin to guess what he was thinking. 'No. That wasn't entertainment. I kissed you because...'

Because why, Rich?

'It was an impulse. A moment. I couldn't walk off that marina without knowing whether the attraction was mutual.'

Given she'd clung to him like a remora, he'd certainly got his answer. Heat billowed up under the collar of her Parks uniform.

'It was,' she murmured. Then she sighed. 'It *is*. I'm awash in candyfloss twenty-four-seven. I'd be sick of it if it didn't smell—' *and feel* '—so good.'

'I'm candyfloss guy?' he breathed. 'I was sure I was earwax.'

He'd eased back on one strong arm so he could

turn his body fully to her for this delicate conversation. It would be so easy to lean forward and find his lips, repeat the experiment, but... to what end? She would eventually run out of things to show him in Coral Bay and then he'd be gone, back to the city, probably for good, and the kissing would be over. And he was right. She wouldn't cope in the city. Not long-term.

'Candyfloss is what I get for...' *attraction* '...for you.'

If Rich was flattered to get a scent all to himself, he didn't show it. He studied her and seemed to glance over her shoulder, his head shaking.

'The timing of this sucks.'

'Would six months from now make a difference?'

'Not a good one,' she thought she heard him mutter.

But he leaned closer, bringing his face within breathing distance, and Mila thought that even though these random kisses confused the heck out of her she could certainly get used to the sensation. Pineapple went quite well with candyfloss, after all. But his lips didn't meet hers; his right shoulder brushed her left one as he leaned beyond her for a moment. When he straightened, he had a flower in his hand, plucked with some of its stem still attached. The delicate pink blossom fanned out around a thatch of golden-pink stamens. On its underside it was paler and waxier, to help it survive the harsh outback conditions.

'One of my favourites,' she said, studying it but not taking it. If she took it he might lean back. 'Desert rose.'

'It matches your lips,' he murmured. 'The same soft pink.'

She couldn't help wetting them; it was instinctive. Rich brushed her cheek with the delicate flower, then followed it with his bare knuckles. Somewhere, harps sang out.

'Pollen,' he explained before folding her fingers around the blossom's thick-leaved stem.

But he didn't move back; he just stayed there, bent close.

'I need you to know something—' he began, a shadow in his gaze.

But no, she wasn't ready to have this amazing day intruded upon by more truths. If it was bad news it could wait. If it wasn't…it could wait too.

'Will you still be here tomorrow?'

He took her interruption in his stride. 'I'm heading back overnight. I have an important meeting at ten a.m.'

Panic welled up like the water in this vent.

Tonight… That was just hours away. A few short hours and he would be gone back to his in-tray, twelve hundred kilometres south of here. After which there were no more reasons for him to return to Coral Bay, unless it was to visit Wardoo, which seemed unlikely given he'd never had the interest before.

And they both knew it.

Mila silenced any more bad news with her fingers on his lips. 'Tell me later. Let's just enjoy today.' Then, when the gathering blue shadows looked as if they weren't going to be silenced, she added, 'Please.'

There wasn't much else to do then than close up the short distance between them again. Mila sucked up some courage and took care of that herself, leaning into the warmth of Rich's cheek, brushing hers along it, seeking out his mouth.

Their kiss was soft and exploratory, Rich brushing his lips back and forth across hers, relearning their shape. She inhaled his heated scent, clung to the subtle smell of *him* through the almost over-powering candyfloss and pineapple that made her head light. He tasted like the chutney in Kip's wife's sandwiches but she didn't care. She could eat pickle for the rest of her days and remember this place. This kiss.

This man.

Long after he'd gone.

'Have dinner with me,' he breathed. 'On the *Portus*. Tonight before I leave.'

Dinner… Was that really what he was asking? Or was he hoping to cap off his northern experience with something more…satisfying? Did she even care? She should… She'd only just begun to get used to the sensations that came with kissing; how could she go from that to something so much more irrevocable in just one evening?

Rich watched her between kisses, his blue eyes peering deeply into hers. He withdrew a little. 'Your mind is very busy…'

This moment would probably be overwhelming for anyone—even those without a superpower. She'd never felt more…normal.

'I'm going out on the water this afternoon,' she

said. 'Come with me. One last visit onto the reef. Then I'll have dinner with you.'

Because going straight from this to dinner to goodbye just wasn't an option.

'Okay,' he murmured, kissing her softly one last time.

She clung to it, to him, then let him go. In the distance, the Land Cruiser honked politely.

'Back to work,' Rich groaned.

Probably just as well. Sitting here on the edge of an ancient sinkhole, older than anything either of them had ever known, it was too easy to pretend that none of it mattered. That real life didn't matter.

She nodded and watched as he pushed to his feet. When he lowered a strong hand towards her she didn't hesitate to slide her smaller fingers into his. The first time ever she didn't give a moment's thought before touching someone.

Pineapple wafted past her nostrils again.

CHAPTER TEN

'ARE YOU KIDDING ME?' Rich gaped at her. 'How dangerous is this?'

'It's got to be done,' Mila pointed out.

Right. Something about baselines for studying dugong numbers. He understood baselines; he worked with them all the time. But not like this.

'Why does it have to be done by *you*?' he pointed out, pretty reasonably he thought, as he did his part in the equipment chain, loading the small boat.

'It's not just me,' she said, laughing. 'There's a whole team of us.'

Yeah, there was. Four big, strong men, experienced in traditional hunting methods. It was the only bit of comfort he got for this whole crazy idea.

'You hate teams,' he pointed out in a low voice. She loved working solo. Just Mila and the reef life. A mermaid and her undersea world.

'I wouldn't do it every day,' she conceded. 'But I'm way too distracted to think about it until it's over. You don't have to come…'

Right. If a gentle thing like Mila could get out there and tackle wild creatures he wasn't about to wuss out. Besides, if anything went wrong he wanted to be there to help make sure she came out of it okay. Finally, those captain-of-the-swim-team skills coming in useful. Though it wasn't likely she'd be doing this in the comfortable confines of Coral Bay's shallows.

The team loaded up the fast little inflatable and all five of them got in—Mila and her ranger quarterbacks—then the documentary crew that were capturing the dugong tagging exercise for some local news channel loaded into their own boat and Rich got in with them. Not close enough, maybe, but as close as he was going to get out on the open water. And the documentary crew would make sure they had a good view of the activities—which meant he would have a good view of Mila's part in it.

I'm just the tagger, she'd said and he'd thought that was a good thing. Until he realised she'd be in the open ocean down the thrashing end of a wild, defensive dugong fitting that tag.

Rich held on as they headed out. The inflatable wasted no time getting well ahead and the film crew did their thing as Rich watched.

'They've spotted a herd,' the documentary producer called to her crew. 'Twenty animals.'

Twenty? Rich swore under the engine noise and his gut fisted. Anything could happen in a herd that size.

As soon as they reached the herd, the little inflatable veered left to cut an animal off the periphery and chase it away rather than drive it into the herd and risk scattering them. Or, worse, hurting them. They ran it in a wide arc for ten minutes, wearing it down, preventing it from re-entering the herd and then he watched as three of the four wetsuit-clad Rangers got to their feet and balanced there precariously as the fourth veered the inflatable across the big dugong's wake. Mila held on for her life in the back of the little boat.

'Get ready!' the producer called to her two camera operators.

Rich tensed too.

When it happened, it all happened in a blinding

flash. The puffed animal came up for a breath, then another, then a third. As soon as they were sure it had a good lungful of air, the first dugong-wrangler leapt over the edge of the inflatable and right onto the dugong's back. The two others followed suit and, though he couldn't quite see what was happening in the thrashing water, he did see Mila toss them a couple of foam tubes, which seemed to help keep the hundred-kilogram dugong incredulously afloat while the men kept its nose, flippers and powerful tail somewhat contained.

Then Mila jumped. Right in there, into that surging white-water of death, with the tracking gear in her tiny hands. Rich's heart hammered almost loud enough to hear over the engine of the documentary boat and he leapt to his feet in protest. Her bright red one-piece flashed now and again above the churning water and kept him oriented on her. The video crew were busy capturing the rest of what was happening, but he had eyes for only one part of that animal—its wildly thrashing back end and Mila where she clung to it, fitting the strap-on tracker to the narrowest point of its thick tail. How that could possibly be the lesser of jobs out there...

She and the dugong both buffeted against the small boat and he realised why they used an inflatable and not a hard shell like the one he was in. Its cushioned impact protected the animal and bounced Mila—equally harm-free—back onto the dugong's tail and helped keep her where she needed to be to finally affix the tracker.

While he watched, they measured the animal in a few key spots and shouted the results to the inflatable's skipper, who managed to scrawl it in a notebook while also keeping the boat nice and close.

Then...all of a sudden, it was over. The whole thing took less than three minutes once the first body hit the water. The aggravated dugong dived deep the moment it was released and the churning stopped, the water stilled and the five bodies tumbling around in its turbulence righted themselves and then swam back to the inflatable. The men hauled Mila in after them and they all fell back against the rubber, their chests heaving. One of the neoprene-suited quarterbacks threw up the stomachful of water he'd swallowed in the melee.

Rich's own heart was beating set to erupt from his chest. He couldn't imagine what theirs were like.

Of all the stupid things that she could volunteer to help with…

Mila fell back against the boat's fat rim and stared up into the blue sky. Then she turned and sought out his boat. His eyes. And as soon as he found them she laughed.

Laughed!

Who was this woman leaping into open ocean with a creature related more closely to an elephant than anything else? What had she done with gentle, mermaid Mila? The woman who took such exquisite care of the creatures on the reef, who didn't even tread on an ant if she could avoid it. Where was all this strength coming from?

He sank back down onto his seat and resigned himself to a really unhappy afternoon. This activity crossed all the boxes: dangerous, deep and—worst of all—totally uncontrollable. Beyond a bit of experience and skill, their success was ninety per cent luck.

It occurred to him for a nanosecond that experience, skill and luck were pretty much everything he'd built his business on.

All in all, they tagged six animals before the team's collective exhaustion called a halt to the effort. Science would glean a bunch of something from this endeavour but Rich didn't care; all he cared about was the woman laid out in the back of the inflatable, her long hair dangling in the sea as the inflatable turned for shore and passed the film crew's boat.

Rich was the first one off when it slid up onto the beach, but Mila was the last one off the inflatable, rolling bodily over its fat edge, her fatigued legs barely holding her up. In between, he stood, fists clenched, bursting with tension and the blazing need to wrap his arms around Mila and never let her go.

Ever.

'Rich!' she protested as he slammed bodily into her, his arms going around to hold her up. 'I'm drenched.'

'I don't care.' He pressed against her cold ear. 'I *so* don't care.'

What was a wet shirt when she'd just risked her life six times over? Mila stood stiffly for a moment but the longer he held onto her, the more she relaxed into his grip and the more grateful she seemed for the strength he was lending her. Her little hands slid up his back and she returned his firm embrace.

Around them, the beach got busy with the packing up of gear and the previewing out of video and the relocation of vessels but Rich just stood there, hugging her as if his life depended on it.

In that moment it felt like absolute, impossible truth.

'Ugh, my legs are like rubber,' Mila finally said, easing back. She kept one hand on his arm to steady herself as her fatigued muscles took back reluctant responsibility for her standing. She glanced up at him where a Mila-shaped patch clung wetly to his chest.

'Your shirt—'

'Will dry.' He saw the sudden goose pimples rising on her skin. 'Which is what you need to be. Come on.'

'I'm not cold,' she said, low, but moved with him up the beach compliantly.

'You're trembling, Mila.'

'But not with cold,' she said again, and stared

at him until her meaning sank in. 'I'm having a carnival moment.'

Oh. Candyfloss.

The idea that his wet skin on hers had set her shivers racing twisted deep down in his guts. He wanted to be at least as attractive to her as she was to him. Though that was a big ask given how keyed-up he was whenever she was around. Yet still his overriding interest was to get her somewhere warm…and safe. Like back into his arms.

That was disturbingly new.

And insanely problematic given he was leaving tonight. And given that he'd vowed to finish the conversation he'd wanted to have out at the sinkhole.

He stopped at their piled-up belongings on the remote beach and plucked the biggest towel out of the pile, wrapping it around her almost twice. He would much rather be her human towel but right now the heat soaked through it was probably more useful to her. She stood for minutes, just letting the lactic acid ease off in her system and walking off the fatigue. Then she passed him the towel and pulled on her shorts and shirt with what looked a lot like pain. She glanced at her team, still packing up all their gear.

'I should help,' she murmured.

Rich stopped her with a hand to her shoulder. 'You're exhausted.'

'So are they.'

'I'm not. I'll help in your place.'

'I'm not an invalid, Rich.'

'No, but it's something I can do to feel useful. I'd like to do this for you, Mila.' When was the last time he'd felt as…impotent…as he had today? Out on that boat, on all that water, witness to Mila risking her life repeatedly while he just…watched. And there was nothing he could do to help her.

It was like sitting in traffic while his father's heart was rupturing.

His glare hit its target and Mila acquiesced, nodding over mumbled thanks.

Rich turned and crossed to help with the mounded pile of equipment from his boat.

He didn't want her gratitude; a heavy hauling exercise was exactly what he needed to get his emotions back in check. The more gear he carried back and forth across the sand, the saner he began to feel—more the composed CEO and less the breathless novice.

Though maybe in this he *was* a novice. It certainly was worryingly new territory.

He was attracted to everything that was soft about Mila—her kindness, her gentleness; even her quirky superpower was a kind of fragile curiosity. Attraction he could handle. Spin out the anticipation and even enjoy. But this...this was something different. This was leaning towards *admiration*.

Hell, today was downright *awe*.

Gentle, soft Mila turned out to be the strongest person he knew, and not just because she'd spent the day wrestling live dugongs. How much fortitude did it take to engage with a world where everyone else experienced things completely differently to you? Where you were an alien within your own community? Every damned day.

So, *attraction* he could handle. *Admiration* he could troubleshoot his way through. *Awe* he would be able to smile and enjoy as soon as the adrenaline spike of today wore off. But there was something else... Something that tipped the scales of his comfort zone.

Envy.

He was coveting the hell out of Mila and her simple, happy, *vivid* life. Amid all the complexity that her remote lifestyle and synaesthesia brought, Mila just stuck to her basic philosophy—protect the reef. Everything else fell into place behind that. Her goals and her strengths were perfectly aligned. No wonder she could curl up in that quirky little stack-house surrounded by all her treasures and sleep deep, long and easy.

When had he ever slept the night through?

When he'd come to Coral Bay on a fact-finding mission, his direction had been clear. Get a feel for the issues that might hamper his hotel development application. The hotel he needed to build to keep the lucrative coastal strip in Wardoo's lease.

Simple, right?

But now nothing was simple. Mila had more than demonstrated the tourism potential of the place but she'd also shown him how inextricably her well-being was tangled up with the reef. They were like a symbiotic pair. Without Mila, the reef would suffer. Without the reef, Mila would suffer.

They were one.

And he was going to put a hotel on her back.

His eyes came up to her as she joined in on the equipment hauling, finding strength from whatever bottomless supply she had. He could yearn like a kid for Mila's simple, focused life and he could yearn like a grown man for her body—but this *need* for her, this *fear* for her... Those weren't feelings that he could master.

And he didn't do powerless. Not any more.

Mila Nakano never was for him. And he was certainly no good for her. If anything, he was the exact opposite of what was good for her.

And he wasn't going to leave tonight without letting her know how much that was true.

CHAPTER ELEVEN

THE *PORTUS* WAS closer by a half-hour than Mila's little stack-house in Coral Bay town centre and, given she was coming to him for dinner anyway, Rich had called his crew up the coast and had the tender pick them both up at the nearest authorised channel in the reef. The last time she'd been aboard she had done everything she could not to touch either of the men wanting to help her board safely; it was probably wrong to feel so much satisfaction at the fact that she didn't even hesitate to put her hand into his now.

Or that she'd looked at him with such trust as he'd helped her aboard.

It warmed him even as it hurt him.

He'd led her into the *Portus'* expansive bow bedroom, piled her up with big fluffy towels, pointed her in the direction of his bathroom and given her a gentle shove. Then he'd folded back the thick, warm quilt on his bed in readiness so that she could just fall into it when she was clean, warm and dry.

That was two hours ago and he'd been killing time ever since, vacillating between wanting to wake her and spend what little time he could with her, and putting off the inevitable by letting her sleep. In the end, he chose sleep and told himself it wasn't because he was a coward. She'd been almost wobbling on her feet as he'd closed the dark bedroom doors behind him; she needed as much rest as he could give her.

Now, though, it was time for Sleeping Beauty to wake. He'd made sure to bang around on boat business just outside the bedroom door in the hope that the sounds would rouse her naturally, but it looked as if she could sleep through a cyclone—*had he ever slept that well in his life?*—so he had to take the more direct approach now.

'Mila?' He followed up with a quiet knock on the door. Nothing.

He repeated her name a little louder and opened the door a crack to help her hear him. Still not so much as a rustle of bedclothes on the other side. He stepped onto the bedroom's thick carpet and took care to leave the door wide open behind him. If she woke to find him standing over her he didn't want it to be with no escape route. He also didn't want it to be *over* her.

'Mila?' he said again, this time crouched down to bed level.

She twitched but little else, and he took a moment to study her. She looked like a child in his massive bed, curled up small, right on the left edge, as though she knew it wasn't her bed to enjoy. As though she was trying to minimise her impact. Or maybe as though she was trying to minimise its impact *on her.* He studied the expensive bedding critically—who knew what association was triggered by the feel of silk against her skin?

Yet she slept practically curled around his pillow. Embracing it. Would she do that if she wasn't at least a little comfortable in this space? She'd been exhausted, yes, but not so shattered that she couldn't have refused if curling up in a bed other than her own had been in any way disturbing to her. There was no shortage of sofas she could have taken instead.

Rich reached out and tucked a loose lock of hair back in with its still-damp cousins. Mila twitched again but not away from him. She seemed to curl her face towards him before burrowing down deeper into his pillow. Actually, his was on the other side of the bed but he would struggle, after he'd left this place, not to swap it for the one Mila practically embraced. Just to keep her close a little longer. Until her scent faded with Coral Bay on the horizon behind him.

He placed a gentle hand on her exposed shoulder. 'Mila. Time to wake up.'

She roused, shifted. Then her beautiful eyes flickered open and shone at him, full of confused warmth as she tried to remember where she was. It only took a heartbeat before she mastered them, though, and looked around the space.

'How did you sleep?' he asked, just to give her an excuse to look back at him.

She pushed herself up, and brought his quilt with her.

'This bed...' she murmured, all sleepy and sexy.

His chest actually hurt.

'Best money could buy,' he squeezed out.

'How do you even get out of it?' Her voice grew

stronger, less dreamy with every sentence she uttered. 'I'm not sure I'm going to be able to.'

That was what he wanted; the kind of sleep the bed promised when you looked at it, lay on it. The kind of sleep that Mila's groggy face said she'd just had. And now that he'd seen his bed with her in it, that was what he wanted too.

But *wanting* didn't always mean *having*.

'Damo will have dinner ready in a half hour,' he said. 'Do you want to freshen up? Maybe come out on deck for some air?'

It was only then that the darkness outside seemed to dawn on her. She pushed up yet straighter.

'Yes, I'm sorry. It was only supposed to be a nap—'

'Don't apologise. After the day you've had, you clearly needed it.' He pushed to his feet. 'I'll see you on deck when you're ready.'

He left her there, blinking a daze in his big bed, and retreated up the steps to the galley, where he busied himself redoing half the tasks his deckhand had already done. Just to keep busy. Just to give Mila the space he figured she would appreciate. He lifted the clear lid on the chowder risotto steaming away beneath it and then, at Damo's frustrated cluck, abandoned the galley, went out on the aft deck and busied himself decanting a bottle of red.

'Gosh, it's even more beautiful at night,' a small voice eventually said from the galley doorway.

His gaze tracked hers across the *Portus'* outer deck. He took it for granted now, but the moody uplights built into discreet places along the gunnel did cast interesting and dramatic shapes along the cat's white surfaces.

'I forget to appreciate it sometimes.'

'Human nature,' she murmured.

But was it? Mila appreciated what she had every single day. Then again, he wasn't at all sure she was strictly human. Maybe all mermaids had synaesthesia.

'What smells so good?'

'No crayfish on the menu tonight,' he assured her. 'I believe we're having some kind of chowder-meets-risotto. What are your feelings about rice?'

Her dark eyes considered that. 'Ambivalent.'

'And clams?'

'Clams are picky,' she said immediately. 'I'm

sure they would protest any use you made of them, chowder or otherwise.'

The allusion brought a smile to his lips. 'But you eat them?'

'Honestly? After today, I would happily eat the cushions on your lovely sofa.'

She laughed and he just let himself enjoy the sound. Because it was the last time he ever would.

He led her to the sofa and poured two glasses of Merlot. 'This isn't going to help much with the sleepiness, I'm afraid.'

Mila wafted the glass under her nose and her eyes closed momentarily. 'Don't care.'

He followed her down onto the luxurious sofa that circled the low table on three sides. Her expression made him circle his glass with liquid a few extra times and sip just a little slower. Craving just a hint of whatever it was that connected Mila so deeply with life.

Pathetically trying to replicate it.

They talked about the dugong tagging—about what the results would be used for and what that meant for populations along this coast. They talked about the coral spawn they'd collected and how little it would take to destroy all that she'd ever collected. One good storm to take out the power for days, one fuel shortage to kill Steve Donahue's generator and the chest freezer they were using would slowly return to room temperature and five years' worth of spawn would all perish. They talked about the two big game fishermen who'd gone out to sea on an ill-prepared boat during the week, and spent a scary and frigid few nights being carried further and further away from Australia on the fast-moving Leeuwin Current before being rescued and how much difference an immediate ocean response unit would have made.

Really he was just raising anything to keep Mila talking.

She listened as well as she contributed and her stories were always so engaging. These were not conversations he got to have back in the city.

He thought that he was letting her talk herself almost out of breath because he knew this might well be the last opportunity he had to do it. But the longer into the night they talked, the more he had to admit that he was letting her dominate their conversation because it meant he didn't have to take such an active part. And if he took a more active part then he knew he would have to begin the discussion he was quietly dreading.

'I'm sorry,' Mila said as she forked the last of the double cream from her dish with the last of her tropical fruit. A gorgeous shade of pink stained her cheeks. 'I've been talking your ear off since the entree.'

'I like listening to you,' he admitted, though *like* wasn't nearly strong enough. But he didn't have the words to describe how tranquil he felt in her presence. As if she were infecting him with her very nature.

That, itself, was warning enough.

'Besides,' he said, beginning what had to be done, 'this might be my last chance.'

Mila frowned. 'Last chance for what?'

'To hear your stories. To learn from you.' Then, as she just stared, he added, 'I have what I need now. There's no reason for me to come back to Coral Bay.'

Yeah, there was. Of course there was. There was Wardoo and there was his proposed development and there was Mila. She was probably enough all by herself to lure him back to this beautiful place. What he meant, though, was that he *wouldn't* be coming back, despite those things.

She just blinked at him as his words sank into her exhausted brain. What kind of a jerk would do this to someone so unprepared?

'No reason? At all?'

He shrugged, but the nonchalance cost him dear. 'I have what I came for.'

It was hard to define the expression that suffused her face then: part-confusion, part-sorrow, part-disappointment. 'What about Wardoo?'

It was impossible not to mark the perfect segue into the revelation he wanted so badly not to make. To hurt this gentle creature in a way that was as wrong as taking a spear gun to some brightly coloured fish just going about its own business on the reef.

But he'd already missed several opportunities to be strong—to be honest—and do the right thing by Mila.

He wasn't about to leave her thinking the best of him.

Not when it was the last thing he deserved.

* * *

'Mila, listen—' Rich began.

'I wasn't making any assumptions,' she said in a rush. 'I know I don't have any claims on you. That I'm necessarily anything more than just…'

Entertainment.

Though the all too familiar and awkward taste of cola forming at the back of her throat suggested otherwise.

*Mila, listen…*was as classic an entrée into the *it's-not-you-it's-me* speech as she'd ever heard. Except she well knew the truth behind that now.

It was *always* her.

Just because she'd found someone that she could be comfortable around—with—didn't necessarily mean Rich felt the same way. Or, even if he did, that it was particularly unique for him. There were probably a lot of women back in the city that he felt comfortable around. More businesslike women with whom he could discuss current affairs. More suitable women that he could take to important functions. More cognitively conventional women that he could just be normal with.

The cola started to transition into the nose-scrunching earwax that she hated so much.

'We've spent days together,' he began. 'We've eaten together and we've kissed a couple of times. It's not unreasonable for you to wonder what we are to each other, Mila.'

He spoke as if he were letting an employee go. Impersonal. Functional. Controlled. It was hard not to admire the leader in him, but it was just as impossible not to resent the heck out of that. He'd clearly had time to prepare for this moment whereas she'd walked into it all sleepy-eyed and Merlot-filled.

Yet, somehow, this felt as prepared as she was ever going to get.

'And what is that, exactly?' she asked.

'There's a connection here,' he said, leaning in. 'I think it would be foolish to try and pretend otherwise. But good chemistry doesn't necessarily make us a good fit.'

She blinked at him. *They* didn't fit? He would fit in anywhere. He was just that kind of a man. Which meant...

'You mean *I'm* not.'

'That's not what I was saying, but you have

to admit that you would fit about as well in my world as I've fit in yours.'

'You fit in mine just fine.' Or so she'd thought.

His laugh wasn't for her. 'The man who can't go in open water? That novelty wouldn't last long.'

She refused to let him minimise this moment. 'Do you not like it here?'

'I didn't say I haven't enjoyed it. I said I don't *fit* here.'

Why? Because he was new to it? 'You haven't really given it much of a chance.'

It was so much easier to defend the place she loved than the heart that was hurting.

Rich sighed. 'I didn't come here looking for anything but information, Mila...'

'Why *did* you come, Rich?' she asked. He'd avoided the question twice before but asking that bought her a few moments to get her thoughts in order. To chart some safe passage out of these choppy emotional waters.

He took a deep, slow breath and studied her, tiny forks appearing between his eyes. Then he leaned forward with the most purpose she'd seen in him and she immediately regretted asking.

'The government is proposing a re-draft of the

boundaries of the leaseholdings on the North-west Cape,' he began. 'They want to remove the coastal strip from Wardoo's lease.'

His words were so unlike the extreme gravity in his face it took her a moment to orient. That was not the terrible blow she'd steeled herself for.

'Why?'

'They want to see the potential of the area ful-filled and remove the impediments to tourism coming in.'

Impediments like the Dawsons protecting the region by controlling the access.

'It's a big deal that this is a World Heritage Ma-rine Park,' he went on. 'They want the world to be able to come see it. But until now they haven't been able to act.'

There was a point in all this corporate speak, somewhere. Mila grappled for it. 'What's changed now?'

'Wardoo's fifty-year lease is up. They're free to renegotiate the boundaries as they wish.'

Ironic that the very listing that was supposed to recognise and protect the reef only made it more attractive for tourists. And all those people needed somewhere to stay.

'And redrawn boundaries are bad?'

'The new leasehold terms will make it nearly impossible to turn a reasonable profit from this land. Without the coastal strip.'

Was she still feeling the effects of her not-so-power nap? Somehow, she was failing to connect the dots that Rich was laying out. 'What has the coastal strip got to do with Wardoo's profitability?'

Rich's broad shoulders lifted high and then dropped slowly as he measured his words.

'Every business that operates in Coral Bay pays a percentage to WestCorp for the opportunity to do so. Tourism has been keeping Wardoo afloat for years.'

The stink of realisation hit her like black tar. She sagged against the sofa back. *That* was why the Dawsons were so staunchly against external developers in Coral Bay.

'So...you weren't protecting the reef,' she whispered. 'You were protecting your profits?'

'WestCorp is a business, Mila. Wardoo is just one holding amongst three dozen.'

She pushed her empty dish away. 'Is that why you were up here? To check up on your tenants?'

It hit her then. 'Oh, God! A percentage of my rent probably goes to you too. You should have said it was a rental inspection, I would have tidied up—'

'Mila—'

She pushed to her feet as her stomach protested the mix of yeast and cherry that came with all the anger and confusion—on top of the clam chowder, red wine and utter stupidity, it threatened a really humiliating resurgence.

'Excuse me, I need a moment.'

She didn't wait for permission. Before Rich could even rise to his own feet, she'd crossed the room and started negotiating the steps down to his bedroom. Once in the spacious en suite bathroom, she braced her hands either side of the sink until she was sure that her churning stomach was not going to actually broil over. Then she pressed a damp cloth to her face and neck until the queasiness eased off.

This was not the first time she'd had synaesthesia-prompted nausea. Her body really couldn't discriminate between actual tastes and imagined, so some combinations, usually reserved for really complicated moments, ended up in long sojourns to a quiet, cool place.

She sagged down onto her elbows on the marble vanity and pressed the cloth to her closed eyes.

If she'd given it any real thought she wouldn't have been surprised to discover Wardoo was getting kickbacks from the local businesses. If they were in the city they'd definitely have been paying rent to someone.

No, the churning cherry was all about how stupid she had been to just assume that Rich would find the *reef* the most valuable part of the Bay. If he liked the reef at all, it was secondary to the income that the tenants could bring him. He was still here for the money.

He was all about the money.

WestCorp is a business, Mila...

He'd even hinted at as much, several times. But she hadn't listened. She and Rich saw the world completely differently. She had no more right to judge him for the way he perceived the world than he had to judge her synaesthesia.

They just came at life from very different places.

Too different.

Leveraging a bunch of cafés and caravan parks

and glass-bottom boat operators for a percentage did not make him a bad person.

It just meant he was no white knight to her reef after all.

She'd have to carry on doing her own white knighting.

She patted her face dry, pinched her cheeks to encourage a little colour into them and switched off the fancy lights as she stepped back into the bedroom. Such a short time ago she'd curled up in that bed—in amongst Rich's lingering scent— and thought drowsily how nice it would be to stay there for ever. Now, that moment felt as dream-like as the past few days.

When viewed with the cold, hard light of reality.

She'd stumbled against Rich's office chair as she'd staggered into the bedroom a few minutes earlier and she took a moment now to right it, sliding it back into the cavity under the work-station and setting to rights the documents she'd splayed across the desktop with her falter. As she did, her eyes slashed across a bound wad of pages that had slipped out from under a plain file.

The word 'Coral Bay' immediately leapt out at her.

She glanced at the empty doorway and then lifted the corner on the cover page like a criminal.

Words. Lots and lots of words. Some kind of summary introduction. She flipped to the next page and saw a map of the coast—as familiar to her as the shape of her own hand. A large area was shaded virtually across the coast road from Nancy's Point.

That was where she stopped being covert.

Mila pulled out the chair, let her wobbly legs sink her into it and unclipped the binder so she could turn the pages more fully. Another plan showing massive trenching down from Coral Bay township—water, power, sewer. Over the page another, showing side elevations of a mass-scale construction—single, two and three storeys high in different places. Swathes of parking. Irrigation. Gardens.

A helipad, for crying out loud.

Her fingers trembled more with every page she turned. Urgent eyes scanned the top of every plan and found the WestCorp logo. Waves of nausea rolled in again and Mila concentrated on slowing her patchy breathing. She bought herself more time by tidying the pages and fixing the binding. Just before she stood, she glanced again at the summary introduction and her eyes fell to the page bottom. An elaborate signature in ink. Rich's signature.

And that was yesterday's date beside it.

The *Portus* seemed to lurch beneath her as if it had been hit by some undersea quake.

Rich was developing the reef—a luxury resort on the coast of Wardoo's land. No wonder he protested the government's plans to excise the coastal strip.

He had *this* under development.

And he'd signed off on it after he'd seen the coral spawn. After he'd first kissed her.

She wobbled to her feet and pressed the incriminating evidence to her chest as she returned to the aft deck. Rich rose politely as she came back out but if he noticed what she was clinging to he showed no sign.

Mila dropped the report on the table between them and let it lie there like some dead thing.

Rich's eyes fell shut briefly, but then found hers

again—one hundred per cent CEO. 'WestCorp isn't a charity, Mila. I have shareholders and other ventures to protect.'

No. That wasn't what he was supposed to protect.

'You're forsaking the reef?' she cut in. 'And the Bay.'

And me, a tiny, hurt voice whimpered.

'I admit it is beautiful, Mila. And diverse. UNESCO obviously agreed to give it World Heritage status. But without the revenue from tourism activity, without the coastal strip, I can't see how I can justify maintaining Wardoo.' His chest rose high and then fell.

Couldn't justify it? Did every part of his world have to pay for itself? Did life itself come with a profit margin?

Her voice fell to a hoarse whisper. 'It's your heritage, Rich. Your roots are here. You're a Dawson. Does that not matter?'

'That's like me saying that your roots are in Tokyo because your surname is Nakano. Do you *feel* Japanese, Mila?'

She'd never fully identified with any one culture in her crazy patchwork quilt family. That

had always been part of her general disconnec-
tion with the world until the day she'd woken up
and realised that where she belonged was *here*.
The reef was her roots. Regardless of the many
where-elses she had come from.

She identified as *Mila*. Wildlife was her people.

And she would defend them against whoever
came.

'You're Saltwater People too, Rich. You just
don't know it. Look at who you become on the
Portus. Look at where you go to find peace.'

'Peace doesn't put food on the table.'

'Does everything have to revolve around the
almighty dollar?'

'We can't all live in shipping containers and
spend our days frolicking with sea life, Mila.
Money matters. Choosing it isn't a bad choice;
it's just not your choice.'

Her beautiful little home had never sounded
so tawdry—nor her job so unimportant—and
when those two things formed at least half of
your world believing in them mattered.

A lot.

She pushed to her feet. Words tumbled up past
the earwax taste of heartbreak and she had to

force them over her tight lips so they could be heard up on the fly bridge. Though there was no chance on earth that the crew hadn't heard their most recent discussion.

'Damo? I would like to go to shore, please.'

Rich rose too. 'Mila, we're not done...'

'Oh, yes. We are.' *Completely.* 'As soon as you're free, Damo.'

There was enough anxiety in her voice to get anyone's attention.

'Mila,' Rich urged, 'you don't understand. If it's not me, it will be someone else...'

'I understand better than you think,' she hissed. 'You used me and you lied to me. About why you were here. About who you are. I squired you around the district like some royal bloody tour and showed you all its secrets, and I thought I was making a difference. I thought you saw the Bay the way I do. And maybe you actually did, yet you're *still* happy to toss it all away with your trenches and your pipes and your helipads.'

Her arms crept around her middle. 'That was my mistake for letting my guard down for you; I won't be so foolish again.'

She stepped up to him as he also rose to his feet.

'But if you think for one minute that I am going to let anyone hurt the place and people that I love, then you—' she pushed a finger into his chest '—don't understand me. I will whip up a PR nightmare for WestCorp. I'll get every single tourist who visits this place to sign my petition and every scientist I know to go on record with the damage that commercialisation does to reefs. You go ahead and throw the Bay to the wolves. You go make your money and spend it on making more money and don't worry about any of us. But I want you to think on something as you sit on your big stockpile of cash, tossing it over your head and letting it rain down on you...'

She flicked her chin up.

'What are you keeping the money for, exactly, if not to allow you to have ten thousand square kilometres of gorgeous, red, barely productive land in your life? Or an ocean. Or a reef. Or a luxury catamaran. Things that might not make any money but are completely priceless because of what they bring you. Money is a means to an end; it's not the end itself. Surely wealth is meaningless unless it buys you freedom or love or—'

She stumbled on the word as soon as it fell

across her lips because she hadn't meant to say it. And she hadn't meant to feel it. But the subtlest undertones of pineapple told her that she did.

Richard Grundy, of all people...

She took a steadying breath.

'Or sanctuary! It won't keep you warm at night and it won't fill the great void inside you that you try so hard to disguise.'

'I don't have a void—'

'Of course you do. You pack your money down into it like a tooth cavity.' She frowned and stepped closer. 'What if wealth is the thing that people like you are raised to believe matters in lieu of the things that actually matter?'

'People like me?' he gritted.

'Disconnected people. Empty people. Lonely people.'

Rich's strong jaw twitched and he paled a little. 'Really, Mila? The poster-child for dysfunction wants to counsel me on being disconnected?'

His hard words hit home, but she could not deny the essential truth in them.

'Has it not occurred to you yet that I am far richer than you could ever be? *Will* ever be? Because I have all of this.' She held her hands out to the moonlight and the ocean and the reef they couldn't see and the wonders they both knew to be on it. 'And I have my *place* within it. The certainty and fulfilment of that. All of this is more wealth than anyone could ever need in a dozen lifetimes.'

Damo appeared at the bottom of the steps down from the bridge, looking about as uncomfortable as she suddenly felt. Here, in this place that she'd already started to think of as a second home.

Mila turned immediately to follow him down to the tender.

'If WestCorp opts not to renew the lease then who knows who would come in or what they might do with it? The only thing that will keep the government from excising the coastal strip is significant capital investment in the area,' he called after her. 'I need to build something.'

She called back over her shoulder. 'Why don't you build an undersea hotel? That would be awesome.'

She refused to think of what she'd seen on his desk as a reasonable compromise. And she refused to let herself believe that the project was still open to amendment, any more than she could believe that *she* made the slightest difference to his secret plans.

He'd *signed* it. In ink.

'Or, better yet, don't build anything. Just let Wardoo stand or fall on its own merits.'

'It will fall.'

'Then give up the lease, if that's what it takes.'

'I don't *want* to give it up. I'm trying to save it.'

She stared at him, her chest heaving. Even he looked confused by that.

'If I surrender the lease,' he went on after the momentary fumble, 'then anyone could take it up. You could end up with a million goats destroying the land. If I keep the lease and don't develop then the government will excise the strip and someone else will come in and do it. Someone who doesn't care about the reef at all.'

'Funny,' she spat. 'I thought that was you.'

For a moment she thought that Rich was going to let her go with the last word still tasting like nail varnish on her lips. But he was a CEO, and people with acronyms for titles probably never surrendered the final word. On principle.

'Mila, don't go. Not like this.'

But final words could sometimes be silent. And

she was determined that hers should be. Besides which, her lungs were too full of the scent of earwax for adequate speech and the last thing she wanted was for Richard Grundy to hear her croak. So she kept moving. Her feet reached the timber dive platform. The jarrah deck's isolation practically pulsed through her feet. Resonating with a kindred spirit, perhaps. She accepted Damo's hand without thought and stepped into the tender, sinking down with her back firmly to the man she'd accepted so readily into her life.

Nothing.

No solo trumpet at Damo's touch. No plinking ball bearings at the breeze rushing under the *Portus*. No fluttering of wings as her skin erupted in gooseflesh.

It was as if every part of her was as deadened as her heart.

Had he not taken enough from her this night? Now he'd muted her superpower.

Behind her, Rich stood silent and still. Had she expected an eleventh-hour apology? Some final sense of regret? An attitudinal about-face?

Just how naive was she, really?

Richard Grundy was making decisions based

on the needs and wants of his shareholders. She couldn't reasonably expect him to put anyone else's needs ahead of his own. And certainly not hers. She was his tour guide, nothing more. A curiosity and an entertainment. A woman he'd known only days in the greater scheme of things. It was pure folly to imagine that she would—or even could—affect any change in his deep-seated attitudes.

Then again, folly seemed to be all Rich thought she was capable of here. In her quaint little shack with her funny little job…

Damo had the good sense to stay completely silent as he ran her back to the marina and dropped her onto the pier. She gave him the weakest of smiles in farewell and didn't wait to watch him leave, climbing down onto the beach and turning towards town. The tide was far enough out that she could wade around the rocks to get back to town and, somehow, it felt critical that she put her feet back in the water, that she prove to herself that Rich had not muted her senses for good.

That he had not broken her.

But there was no symphony as the water swilled around her bare feet. And as she turned to look out to the reef, imagining what was down there, there was no sound or sensation at all.

Everything was as deadened as her heart.

It was impossible to imagine a world without her superpower to help her interpret it. Or without her reef to help her breathe. And, though she hated to admit it after such a spectacularly short time, she was struggling to even imagine a world without Rich in it.

To help her live.

How had he done that? So quickly. So deeply. And—knowing what he'd done—how could she ever trust any of her senses ever again?

CHAPTER TWELVE

'I'VE GOT NEWS,' her supervisor said down the telephone, his voice grave. 'But you're not going to like some of it.'

Mila took a deep breath. There had been much about the past nine weeks that she didn't like, least of all her inability to get the treacherous Richard Grundy completely from her mind. Whether she was angry at herself for failing to heed her own instincts or angry at him for turning out to be such a mercenary, she couldn't tell.

All she knew was that time had not healed that particular wound, no matter what the adage promised. And no matter how many worthy distractions she'd thrown at it.

It was her own stupid fault that many of her favourite places were now tainted with memories of Rich in them. She had to go showing them off...

'Go ahead, Lyle.'

'First up… Wardoo's lease has been renewed.'

Her stomach clenched. *Renewed*, Lyle had said. Not *refilled*.

Part of the emotional swell she'd been surfing these past months—up, down, up, down—was due to the conflict between wanting Rich to keep his heritage and wanting him to surrender his resort plans. If Rich kept Wardoo it meant he must have kept the coastal strip, which meant going ahead with the resort. But if he dropped the resort, it meant he must have given up Wardoo. And giving up Wardoo meant there was no conceivable reason for Rich to ever be in Coral Bay again.

So, secretly craving an opportunity to see Rich again meant secretly accepting commercialisation of her beloved coast.

'By the Dawsons?'

How her stomach could leap quite that high while still fisted from nerves she didn't know but it seemed to lurch almost into her throat, accompanied by the delicious hot chocolate of hope behind her tongue.

'Looks like they're staying.'

He's staying. Impossible to think of Wardoo as WestCorp's. Not when she'd eaten sandwiches with and stood in the living room with—and *kissed*—the the man who owned it.

'I'm looking at a copy of an agreement that I'm probably not supposed to have,' Lyle admitted. 'Friends in high places. It's not the whole thing, just highlights.'

'And the coastal strip?'

Please… There was still a chance that Rich had negotiated a different outcome. That he'd dropped the resort plans. Or that he'd found a way to keep Wardoo profitable without the coastal strip.

Not the perfect outcome, but one she only realised in this moment that she would accept. As long as it wasn't *Rich* trashing her reef…

'It's staying in the leasehold,' Lyle admitted and her heart sank. 'Not without conditions, though. That's what I want to talk to you about.'

She'd been the one to tell her boss about the government's plans for the coastal strip, but she never told him about Rich's development. Or that she was on a first name basis with the Dawsons.

The hopeful hot chocolate wavered into a cigarettey kind of mocha.

'What kind of conditions?' she asked suspiciously. Though, really, she knew.

The helicopters were probably circling Coral Bay right now, waiting for that helipad.

'Government has approved a development for the Bay,' he said.

Courtesy of a two-month head start, that news didn't send her to water, but it still hurt hearing it. Had she really imagined he would change his multi-million-dollar plans…?

For her?

The hot chocolate completely dissipated and Mila wrapped the arm not holding the phone around her middle and closed her eyes. She asked purely because she was not supposed to already know.

'What kind of development, Lyle?'

'Like I said, I've only got select pages,' he started. 'But it's big, some kind of resort or hotel. Dozens of bathrooms or kitchens; it's hard to tell. No idea why they'd need quite that many, so far from the accommodation,' Lyle flicked through pages on his end of the phone, 'but there's lots of that too. Looks like a theatre of some kind, and a massive wine cellar, maybe? Underground, any-way, temperature-controlled. And a helipad of all things. It's hard to say what it is. But it's not small, Mila. And it can't be a coincidence that it's coming up just as Wardoo's lease is resolved.'

No. It was no coincidence.

'Do you know where it's approved for?' she breathed.

This was her last hope. Maybe he'd shifted its site further south, out of the Marine Park. Though really, wouldn't that defeat the purpose?

'There is a sketch map. Looks like it's about a half-hour south of you. Nancy's Point, maybe?'

Ice began to crystallise the very cells in her flesh.

So it was done. And at his great-grandmother's favourite point, of all places.

'Lyle, look through the documents. Is there any reference to a company called WestCorp anywhere in them?'

Lyle shuffled while Mila died inside.

'Yeah, Mila. There is a WestCorp stamp on one of the floor plans. Who are they?'

Mila stared at the blank space on the wall opposite her.

'WestCorp is the Dawsons,' she breathed down the line.

Lyle seemed as speechless as she was. 'Dawsons? You're kidding. They're the last ones I would have thought—'

'We don't know them,' Mila cut in. 'Or what they're capable of. They're just a family who loved this land once. They haven't lived here for decades.'

'But still—'

'They're not for the reef any more, Lyle.' She realised she was punishing him for Rich's decisions. 'I'm sorry, I have to go. Can you send me those documents?'

This time his hesitation was brief. 'I can't, Mila. I'm not even supposed to have seen them. This was just a heads-up.'

Right. Like a five-minute warning siren that a tsunami was coming. What was she supposed to do with that?

'I understand,' she murmured. 'And I appreciate it. Thank you, Lyle.'

It took no time to lock up her little office and get into her four-wheel drive. Then about a half-hour more to get down to Nancy's Point, half expecting to see site works underway—survey pegs, vehicle tracks, a subterranean wine cellar. But there was nothing, just the same rocky outlook she'd visited a hundred times. The place Rich had first come striding towards her, his big hand outstretched.

Impotence burned as bourbon in her throat. She tried to imagine the site filled with tourists, staff, power stations and treatment plants and found she couldn't. It was simply inconceivable.

And in that moment she decided to tell Rich so.

If she didn't fight for her reef, who would?

There had been no communication between them since he'd left all those weeks ago but this was worth the precedent—now that it was a reality. But she wasn't brave enough to talk to him face to face or even voice to voice. A big part of her feared what it would do to her heart to hear his voice right inside her ear, and what it would do to her soul to have to endure his justification for this monstrosity. She had a smartphone and she had working fingers, and she could tap him one heck of a scathing email telling him exactly what she thought of his plans to put a resort at Nancy's Point. And she could do it right now while she was still angry enough to be honest and brave.

Brave in a way she hadn't been when she'd fled the *Portus* that night.

She climbed back into her car and reached into her dashboard for her phone, then swiped her way through to her email app. She gave a half-moment's consideration to a subject line that he couldn't ignore and then began tapping on letters.

Subject: Nancy will turn in her grave!

'All right, folks, time to get wet!'

Mila sat back and let the excited tourists leap in ahead of her. If they'd been nervous earlier, about snorkelling in open ocean, the anxiety dissipated completely when they spotted their first whale shark, the immense shape looming as a shadow in the water ahead. There were two out here, but the boat chose this one to centre on while another vessel chugged their passengers closer to the other one. But not too close…there were rules. It was up to the tourists to swim the distance and close up the gap between them.

Not everyone was a natural swimmer and so every spare member of crew got in the water with them and shepherded a small number of snorkelers each. Each leader took an underwater whiteboard so they could communicate with their group without having to get alongside them or surface constantly. Easier when you were navigating an animal as big as a whale shark to be able to keep your eyes on its every move.

The last cluster slipped off the back of the boat and into the open water in an excited, splashy frenzy.

That left Mila to go it alone—just how she liked it. She'd eased herself right out onto the front of the big tourist boat where none of them thought to go and so she hadn't had to sit amongst them with the smells and sounds of unfamiliar people. Now, she gave the captain a wave so he knew she was in, and slid down quietly and gently into the silken water.

It was normally completely clear out here, barring the odd cluster of weed floating along or balls of fish picking at the surface, but the churning engines of two boats and the splashing of the associated snorkelling tourists made the water foggy with a champagne of bubbles in all directions. Easy to forget what was out here with them when she couldn't see it, but Mila swam a wide arc to break out of the white-water. As the boats backed away from the site, the water cleared, darkened and then settled a little. The surface turbulence still rocked her but, with her head under, it was much calmer. Calm enough to get on with the job. She looked around her at the light streaming down into the deep blue, converging on some distant point far below, her eyes hunting for the creature so big it seemed impossible that it could hide out here.

The first clue that it was with them was the frenzied flipper action of the nearby tourists, then a great looming shape materialised in slow motion out of the blue below them straight towards her. The whale shark's camouflage—the very thing she'd come to photograph—made it hard for Mila to define its distinctive shape until it was nearly upon her, but it did nothing more dramatic than cruise silently by, its massive tail fanning just once to propel it the entire distance between the other tourists and her group. Everyone else started swimming to keep up with it while Mila back-pedalled madly to get herself out of its way.

She dived under as it passed her, and she got a good view of the half-dozen remoras either catching a ride on the shark's underside or using its draught to swim against its pale underbelly. She swung her underwater camera up and took a couple of images of the patterning around its gills—the ones that the star-mapping software needed—and then watched it disappear once again into the deep blue. But she knew it wouldn't be gone long. Whale sharks seemed to enjoy the interaction with people and this one circled around and emerged out of nothing again to swim between them once more. Mila photographed it on the way back through in case it wasn't the same one at all, then set off after its relaxed tail, swimming back towards the main group of tourists. Two boatloads were combined now, all eager to see the same animal.

As she approached, a staff member in dive gear held up a whiteboard with four letters on it.

R U OK?

Mila gave him an easy thumbs-up and he turned and focused on the less certain swimmers. It was more exhausting than many expected, being out here in the open current and trying to swim clear of a forty-foot-long prehistoric creature.

Mila let herself enjoy the shark, the gorgeous light filtering down through the surface and the

sensations both brought with them. She attributed whale sharks with regal qualities—maybe
her most literal association yet—and this one was
quite the prince. Comparatively unscarred, spectacular markings, big square head, massive gaping mouth that swallowed hundreds of litres of
seawater at a time. When it wasn't gulping, it
pressed its lips together hard to squeeze the head-
ful of water out through its gills and then swallow
what solids were left behind in its massive mouth.
To Mila, the lips looked like a vaguely wry smirk.

Her chest squeezed and not because of exertion.

She'd seen that smirk before. But not for months.

She back-swam again, to maintain the required
safety distance, and watched the swimmers on
the far side of the animal move forward as it
swam away from them. Another carried a whiteboard, but he wasn't a diver and he wasn't in one
of the company wetsuits. Mila tipped her head
and looked closer.

The snorkeler wrote something on his board
with waterproof marker then held it aloft in the
streaming light.

NOT...

She had to wait for the long tail of the whale shark to pass between them before she could read it properly.

NOT EN SUITES... LABS.

What? What did that mean? She straightened to read it again, certain she'd misread some diving instruction. The man wiped it off with his bare arm and wrote again. Something about the way he moved made her spine ratchet straighter than even the circling whale shark did. But she could not take her eyes off his board. He held it up again and the words were longer and so the letters were smaller. Mila had to swim a little closer to read them.

ROOMS NOT 4 TOURISTS.
4 RESEARCHERS.

Her heart began to pound. In earnest. She tried to be alert to what the shark was doing but found it impossible to do anything other than stare at that whiteboard and the man holding it.
'Rich?'
She couldn't help saying it aloud and the little word must have puffed out of the top of her snor-

kel into the air above the surface to be lost on the stiff ocean breeze.

He held the board up again, the words newly written.

NOT U/GROUND WINE CELLAR...

The whale shark swam back through between them, doing its best to drag her eyes off the man wiping the board clean again and back onto the *true* ocean spectacle, but Mila paid it no heed, other than to be frustrated by the spectacular length of the shark as it blocked her view of Rich. As soon as it passed, she read the two words he'd replaced on the board. Her already tight breath caught altogether.

SPAWN BANK.

She pushed her feet and gasped for air above the surface. Water splashed and surged against her body, buffeting her on two sides. Using the clustered snorkelers for reference, she stroked her way towards them with already weary muscles. Just out of voice range, another snorkeler rose above the splash. The only head other than hers poking out of the water while the massive shark dominated attention below.

Rich.

They swam directly towards each other, oblivious to any monsters of the deep still doing graceful laps below them. But when they got close, Mila pulled up short and slid her mask up onto her head.

'What are you doing here?' Her arms and legs worked in opposition to keep her stable in the undulating water.

'I got your email,' Rich answered, raising his mask too. His thick hair spiked up in all directions.

'You could have just replied,' she gasped as the gently rolling seas pitched her in two directions at once.

Rich swam a little closer and Mila turned to keep some distance between them. As life-preserving as the four metres' clearance she was supposed to give the whale shark. They ended up swimming in a synchronised arc in the heaving swell, circling each other.

'Yeah, I could have. But I wanted to see you.'

Hard enough to speak as all her muscles focused on keeping her afloat without the added complication of a suddenly collapsing chest cavity.

She didn't waste time with coyness. 'Why? To break the news in person?'

His voice was thick as he answered. 'It's not a resort, Mila. It's a technology centre. The Wardoo Northern Studies Centre.'

Labs. Accommodation for researchers.

Incongruous to smell hot chocolate over the smell of fresh seawater and marine diesel, but that was hope for you…

'It has a helipad, Rich.'

He ignored her sarcasm and answered her straight. 'For a sea rescue chopper.'

She just blinked. Hadn't they talked about that the night on the *Portus*? The difference it would make to lives up here?

Her voice was as weak as her breath, suddenly. 'And the spawn bank?'

'Subterranean. Temperature-controlled. Solar-powered. You can't keep that stuff in a fish freezer, Mila. It's too important.'

She circled him warily in the water.

'Why?'

There it was again. Such a simple little word but it loomed as large as the whale shark now swimming away in the distance.

A wave splashed Rich full in the face. 'Is this really where you want to have this discussion?'

'You picked it,' she pointed out.

Mila could see all the tourists making their way back to their respective boats, ready to go and find another shark at another location. But, in the distance between them, she saw something else. The flashing white double hull of the *Portus.* Poised to whisk Rich away from her once again.

He puffed, as the swell bobbed them both up and down.

'A state-of-the-art research and conference fa-cility appealed to the government's interest in improving the region.' He swam around her as he spoke but kept his eyes firmly locked on hers. Effort made every word choppy. 'It satisfies the need for facilities for all the programmes run-ning up here.'

The scientists, the researchers. Even the cavers. They would all have somewhere local to work now.

She wanted to reply but didn't. Breathing was

hard enough without wasting air on pointless words. Besides which, she didn't trust herself to speak just yet.

His eyes darted to the *Portus*, to his sanctuary, but it was too far away to provide him with any respite now. 'They didn't have the funding for something like that; it had to be private investment.'

And who else was going to invest in a region like this for something like that, if not a local?

Mila lifted her mouth above the waterline. 'I can't imagine Wardoo will ever make enough to pay for a science centre. Even with kickbacks from your tenants.'

'The centre should pay for itself eventually. With grants. And conference business. The emergency response bit, WestCorp will be covering.'

His breath-stealing revelation was interrupted by the burbling arrival of Mila's charter boat alongside them; it towered above and dozens of strangers' eyes peered over the edge at them. Rich passed the little whiteboard back to whoever he had borrowed it from and waited until she was able to scrabble aboard the dive platform. Gravity immediately made its presence felt in muscles that had been working so hard to keep her afloat and away from the whale sharks. Rich had a quick word with the crew and the charter chugged happily over to the *Portus* and waited as they transferred from one dive deck to the other.

Moments later, the twenty curious tourists were happily heading off after another whale shark sighting signalled by Craig in his Cessna high above them.

A science centre. Rich was planning on building an entire facility so that all the work being done on the reef could be done locally, properly and comfortably. No more long-haul journeys. No more working out of rust-flecked transportables or four-wheel drives. No more vulnerable, fish-filled freezers for her spawn. The researchers of Coral Bay would have facilities at least as good as the visitors who flocked here in the high season.

It was a godsend in so many ways.

But Rich has used it to buy his way to holding onto the revenue-rich coastal strip, a flat inner voice reminded her.

He could have just freed himself of Wardoo and run, a perkier voice said. *He didn't have to come back.*

Is he even 'back'? the cynical voice said. *He's owned and run it for years without ever setting foot on the property. You still might never see him again.*

I'm seeing him now, aren't I...?

Yes. She was. Fulfilling her most secret hopes. The ones she'd pushed down and down until the only place they could be expressed was in her dreams. Mila stripped off her mask and snorkel and dropped them on the dive deck but left her flippered feet dangling in the deep.

Ready for a fast getaway.

'Do you even want Wardoo?' she challenged without looking at him.

'I thought I didn't,' he admitted, casting the words to the sea like she had. 'Not if I couldn't make it profitable. I thought it was just a business like any other to me. A means to an end. A millstone even.'

'But it's not?'

'Turns out I'm more northern than I thought,' he quipped. 'I didn't know how much until that night on the *Portus*. After we'd been there and I was able to conceptualise what I'd be losing.'

Mila studied her waving fins in the undulating water below the *Portus.*

'Wardoo was an emotional sanctuary when my mother died, and I'd forgotten how much. I let myself forget. I painted a picture of what it could be—full of children, full of love—and all of that came rushing back when I faced the reality of losing it. That's why I was reluctant to go out there; I feared it wouldn't make my decision any easier.'

She remembered his quietness at Jack's Vent. Were those the thoughts he'd been struggling with?

'And what about the reef?' she pressed. 'How was discovering that going to help you make your decision?'

'I needed to know what I was up against with the development. See it as the government sees it.'

'Sure.' She looked sideways at him. 'Who better to ask than a government employee?'

'I wasn't expecting you, Mila. Someone with your passion and connectedness. I thought I was just getting a guide to show me around. I didn't mean to exploit your love for the reef.'

'Okay, so you're sorry. Is that what you came all this way to say?'

Rich frowned. 'You likened Wardoo to the *Portus*, that last day I saw you,' he said. 'And I spent a lot of time thinking about that, of all the reasons it wasn't true. Except that, eventually, I realised it was. I don't hesitate to let other areas of WestCorp's operations pay for maintaining and running the *Portus* because she's become a fundamental part of my survival. She makes me…happy. She's important.'

'Except the land isn't important to you,' she reminded him.

He found her eyes. Stared. 'It is to you.'

A whale shark bumping up against her legs couldn't have rocked her more. Cherry-flavoured confusion whirled in her head.

'You signed a fifty-year lease—' she grappled '—you're building an entire science and rescue facility. You're changing all your big corporate plans…to please *me*? Someone you've known for a few days at most?'

No. There had to be another angle here. Some kind of money trail at work.

Rich turned side on to face her.

'Mila, you have a handle on life that I'm only beginning to understand. You are just…in tune. You dive into life with full immersion. Before I met you I would have scoffed at how important that was in life. I'm pretty sure I did scoff at it, until I saw it in action. In *you*.' He brought them closer, but still didn't touch her. 'I envy what you have, Mila. And I absolutely don't want to be the one to take it from you.'

Uneasiness washed around them.

'You're not responsible for me, Rich,' she said tightly.

'I don't feel responsible, Mila. I feel…grateful.' He swung his legs up under him and pushed to standing. 'Come on, let's get warm.'

She was plenty warm looking up at all that hard flesh, thanks very much.

Without accepting his aid, she also stood and used the short, arduous climb up the *Portus'* steps to get her thoughts in order. On deck, Rich patted at his face and shoulders with one of the thick towels neatly piled there.

'I'm a king in the city, Mila. Well-connected, well-resourced. I have colleagues and respect and a diary full to overflowing with opportunity.

Busy enough to mask any number of voids inside. But you called me empty and disconnected—' *and lonely* '—and you named all the things I'd started to feel so dramatically when I came here. To this place where none of those city achievements meant squat. A place that stripped me back to the essence of who I am. I hated being that exposed because it meant I couldn't kid myself any more.'

'About what?'

He tucked himself deeper into the massive towel.

'Losing my mother so young hit me hard, Mila. Being sent away to school just added to that. I was convinced then that if I played by life's rules then I would be rewarded with the certainty that had just been stripped away from me. The rules said that if you worked hard you would be a success, and that with success came money and that people with money got the power.'

'And you wanted power?' she whispered.

'As a motherless eight-year-old abandoned in boarding school? Yes, I did. I never wanted life to happen *to* me again.'

Mila could only stand and stare. 'Did it work?'

'Yeah, everything was going great. All my sacrifices were paying off and I was rising through the ranks nicely. And then my father's heart ruptured one day while I was busy taking an international conference call and I couldn't get there in time and he died alone. Life stuck it to me, just to remind me it could. So I worked harder and I earned more. I forsook everything else and I stuck it back to life.'

'And did *that* work?' she breathed, knowing the answer already.

Rich slid her a sideways look and it was full of despair. 'I thought so. And then I came here. And I met you and I saw how you didn't need to compete with life because you just worked with it. Symbiotically. Like the creatures on the reef you told me about with all their diversity, working together, cooperatively. You *owned* life.'

Rich looked towards the coastline—burnished red against the electric blue of the coastal reef lagoons.

'I don't own it, Rich. I just live it. As best I can.'

'I'd worked my whole life to make sure that *I* got life's best, Mila. I upskilled and strategised and created this sanitised environment where everything that happened to me happened *because* of me. Not because of someone else and sure as heck not because of capricious life! And then I discover that you're just getting it organically... just by being you.'

'Rich...'

'This is not a complaint, Mila. Just an explanation. I got back to Perth and I was all set to go ashore for that critical ten a.m., and then it hit me, right between my eyes.'

'What did?'

'That I didn't want to be a Grundy any more.'

Mila frowned. 'What do you want to be?'

His brows dipped and then straightened. His blue eyes cleared and widened with resolve. 'I think I want to be a Dawson.'

She gasped.

'*The* Dawson—the one you described to me that first day we met and spoke of with such respect. Protector of the reef. Part of the land up here. Part of the history. I want you to look at me like someone who built something here, not just...mined it for profits.'

She realised. 'That's why you wanted to keep the Wardoo lease?'

'Now I just have to learn how to run it.'

Mila thought through the ramifications of his words. 'You'd give up WestCorp?'

He shook his head. 'I'll transform it. Play to my own strengths and transition away from the rest. Get back to fundamentals.'

Nothing was quite as fundamental as grazing the animals that fed the country.

'You have zero expertise in running a cattle station,' she pointed out.

'I have expertise in buying floundering businesses and building them back up. That's how WestCorp got its start. About time I applied that to our oldest business, don't you think? See what it could be with some focus. Besides, as you so rightly pointed out, I have minions. Very talented minions.'

She could see it. Rich as a Dawson. Standing on Wardoo's wrap-around verandas, a slouch hat shielding him from the mid-morning sun, even if it was only once a month. But she wasn't in that picture. And, despite saying all the right things, he wasn't inviting her.

This was just a *mea culpa* for everything that had gone down between them. Nothing more.

'If anyone can do it,' she murmured, 'you can.'

Her heart squeezed just to say it. Having him be twelve hundred kilometres away was hard enough. Having him here in Coral Bay yet not *be* with him would be torture. But she'd done hard things before. And protecting herself was second nature.

'Nancy would be proud of you, Rich.'

It was impossible not to feel the upwelling of happiness for him; that this good man had found his way to such a good and optimistic place.

'I'm glad someone will because the rest of my world is going to be totally and utterly bemused. I'm going to need your help, Mila,' he said, eyes shining. 'To make a go of it.'

Earwax flooded her senses. She knew he didn't mean to be cruel, but what he asked... It was too much. Even for a woman who had hardened herself against so much in the past. She couldn't put herself through that.

She wouldn't.

He would have to find someone else to be his cheer squad as he upturned his life.

'You don't need me,' she said firmly. 'Now that you know what you want to do.'

Confusion stained his handsome face. 'But you're the one that inspired me.'

'I'm not some kind of muse,' she said, pulling her hair up into something resembling a soggy ponytail. 'And I'm not your staff.'

He reeled back a little. 'No. Of course. That's not what I—'

Tying up her hair was like breathing to her—second nature. Yet she couldn't even manage that with her trembling hands. She abandoned her effort and clenched them as the smell of processed yeast overruled the heartbreak.

'I recognise that I'm a curiosity to you and that my *quirky* little life here is probably adorably idyllic from your perspective, particularly at a time when you're facing some major changes, but I never actually invited you to share it. And I'm not obliged to, simply because you've had an epiphany about your own life.'

Rich frowned. Stared. Realised.

'I've lost your faith,' he murmured.

'It's been nine weeks!' Anger made her rash but it was pain that made her spit. 'And you just roll up out of the blue wanting something from me yet again. Enough to even hunt me down two kilometres off—'

She cut herself off on a gasp. *Offshore*...

'You were in the deep!' she stammered. 'Way beyond the drop-off.'

Rich grimaced. 'I was trying not to think about it.'

'You came out into the open ocean to find me.' Where life was utterly uncontrollable. 'With sharks and whales and…and…'

'Sea monsters,' he added helpfully.

Maybe that was her cue to laugh. Maybe that would be the smart thing to do—laugh it off and move on with her life. But Rich had gone *into the deep*. Where he never, ever went.

The yeast entirely vanished, to make way for a strong thread of pineapple.

Love.

The thing she'd been struggling against since the day she'd sat, straddled between his thighs, on the sea kayak on Yardi Creek. The thing she'd very determinedly not let herself indulge since the night she'd motored away from him all those weeks ago.

No one had ever put themselves into danger for

her. Or even vague discomfort. All her life *she* was the one who'd endured unease for the ease of others.

Yet Rich had climbed down into the vast unknown of open water and swum with a whale shark…

And he'd done it to get to *her.*

'Why are you really here, Rich?' she whispered.

He'd apologised.

He'd had an epiphany…all over the place.

But he hadn't told her why he'd come in person.

He studied her close, eyes tracking all over her face, and she became insanely self-conscious about what she must look like, fresh out of the water with a face full of mask pressure marks.

'I have something for you, Mila.' He reached for another towel and carefully draped it around her shoulders, tucking it into her cold hands. 'Come on.'

He discarded his own towel and Mila padded silently into the galley behind him as he crossed to a shelf beside the interior sofa and tucked something there into his fist. Gentle hands on her shoulders urged her down onto the sofa as he squatted in front of her. All that bare flesh and candyfloss was incredibly distracting.

'I should have reached out to you, Mila,' he started. 'Not left it nine weeks.' His eyes dropped to his fist momentarily, as though to check that whatever was in there was *still* in there. 'But it took me half of that to get my head around the things that you'd said. To get my head right.'

That still left several weeks...

'And then I didn't want to come back to you until I had something tangible to offer you. Development permission on the Northern Studies Centre. A plan. Something I could give you that would show how much I—'

His courage seemed to fail him just at the crucial moment. He blew a long, slow breath out and brought his gaze back to hers.

'This is harder than stepping into that ocean,' he murmured, but then he straightened. 'I don't have planning approval to give you, Mila. That's still a week or two away. But I have this. And it's something. A place-holder, if you like.'

He opened his white-knuckled hand to reveal a small silk pouch.

Mila stared at it and the tang of curiosity added

itself to all the pineapple to create something almost like a delicious cocktail.

'What is it?'

'A gift. An apology.' He took a deep breath, hand outstretched. 'A promise.'

That word stalled her hand just as it hovered over the little pouch. But he didn't expand on it, just held his palm flat and not quite steady.

That made her own shake anew.

But the pouch opened easily and a pale necklace slid out. A wisp of white-gold chain and hanging from it...

'Is that your pearl?'

The one from the oyster stacks that day. The one she'd given him as a memento of the reef. The one that was small and a little bit too malformed to be of actual value.

It hung on its cobweb-fine chain as if it was as priceless as any of its more perfect spherical cousins.

More so because it came from Rich.

'It's your pearl,' he murmured. 'It always was.'

She lifted her eyes to his.

'I should have known better than to try and stage-manage this whole reunion,' he said. 'I guess I have a way to go in giving up control over uncontrollable things.'

Her heart thumped even harder.

This was a *reunion*?

Her eyes fell back to the pearl on its beautiful chain. 'But I gave this to you.'

He nodded. 'To remember you by. I would rather have the real deal.'

She stared at him, wordless.

'I know you've done it tough in the past,' he went on. 'That you consider yourself as much a misfit as your grandmother. And I know that's made it hard for you to trust people. Or believe in them. But you believed in me when we met and I came to hope that maybe you trusted me a little bit too.'

Still she could do nothing but stare. And battle the myriad incompatible tastes swamping the back of her throat and nose.

'I'm hoping we can get that back. With time. And a fair amount of effort on my part.'

'You lied to me, Rich.' There was no getting around that.

'I was lying to me, too. You raised too many

what-ifs in my nice ordered life, Mila. And I didn't deal in ifs, I only dealt in certainties.'

Did he mean to use the past tense?

'You threw into doubt everything I'd been raised to believe, and I…panicked. I fell back on what I knew best. And what I started to feel for you… It was as uncontrollable as everything I'd ever fought against.'

'You said your world was in the city,' she whispered. Saying it aloud was too scary because what if she reminded him? What if she talked him out of what she was starting to think he was saying?

But she had to know.

And he had to say it.

'That's because I had no idea then that you were about to become my world,' he attested. 'My world is wherever you are.'

Pineapple suffused every other scent trying to get her attention. But every other scent had no chance. Not while she sat here, so near to a half-naked Rich with truth in his eyes and the most amazing miracle on his gorgeous lips.

'We barely know each other.'

Did she need to test him again? Or did she just not trust it?

Rich leaned closer. 'I know everything I need to know about you. And you have a lifetime to get to know me better.'

'What exactly are you saying?'

'I'm saying that you can swim Wardoo's sink-hole whenever you want. And you can use the *Portus* any time you need a ride somewhere. And you'll have your own swipe key for the Science Centre and sole management of the spawn bank.'

He forked his fingers through her hair either side of her face.

'I'm saying that you have a standing welcome in any part of my life. I'm through putting impediments of any kind between myself and the most spectacularly unique and beautiful woman I could ever imagine meeting. I'm saying that your synaesthesia does not entertain me or confuse me or challenge me. It delights me. It reminds me what I've been missing in this world.' His fingers curled gently against her scalp to punctuate his vow. 'I will make it my life's work to understand it—and you—because the Dawson kids are probably going to have it and I'd like them to always feel loved and supported, even by their poor, superpower-deficient dad.'

Dawson *kids*?

Her heart was out-and-out galloping now.

'I'm saying that all of this will happen on *your* schedule, as soon as I've won back your trust and faith in me. You and I are meant to be together, Mila. I don't think it's any coincidence that we first met at a place that was so special to my great-grandmother. Nancy had my back that day.'

He pressed his lips against hers briefly.

'I'm asking you to be with me, Mila Nakano. To help me navigate the great unknown waters ahead. To help me interpret them.' Then, when she just stared at him, still wordless, he added, 'I'm saying that I love you, Mermaid. Weirdness inclusive. In fact, especially for that.'

Mila just stared, overcome by his words, and by the pineapple onslaught that swamped her whole system. It seemed to finally dawn on Rich that she hadn't said a word in a while.

A very long while.

'Have I blown it?' he checked softly, setting himself back from her. 'Misjudged your interest?' She still didn't speak but he braved it out. 'Or am I the creepiest stalker ever to live, right now?'

Mila caressed the smooth undulations of the

imperfect pearl resting in her fingers. Grounding herself. She traced the fine chain away from it and then back again. But the longer she did it, the clearer the pearl's personality became.

Rich's soft voice broke into her meditation.

'Is that a happy smile or a how-am-I-going-to-let-him-down-gently smile?'

She found his nervous eyes.

'It's the pearl,' she breathed. 'My subconscious has finally given them a personality.'

'Oh.' The topic change seemed to pain him, but he'd just promised not to rush her. 'What is it?'

Maybe her subconscious had been waiting for him all this time so that she'd know it when she saw it. 'Smitten.'

Her cotton candy stole back in as a cautious smile broke across Rich's face.

'Smitten is a good start,' he said, nodding his appraisal. 'I can work with smitten.'

'You won't need to. It's a small pearl,' she murmured on a deep, long breath. 'It only reflects a small percentage of what I'm feeling.'

This time, the hope in Rich's expression was so palpable it even engendered a burst of hot chocolate on his behalf.

Well, that was a first.

'Mila, you're killing me...'

'Payback.' She smiled, then slipped the pearl chain around her neck and fiddled with the clasp until it was secure. Made him wait. Made him sweat, just a little bit. After nine weeks, it was the least she could do.

And after a lifetime of strict caution, it was almost the best she could do.

'It killed me to walk away from you the last time I was on the *Portus*,' she said. 'I'm not doing it again. I may need to take things slow for a bit, but—' she took a deep breath '—yes, I would love to explore whatever lies ahead. With you,' she clarified, to be totally patent.

Rich hauled her to her feet and whipped the massive towel from around her until it circled him instead. Then he brought her right into its fluffy circle, hard up against him, and found her mouth with his own.

'I think I first fell for you during the coral spawn,' Rich murmured around their kisses. 'Literally in the middle of the snow globe. And then the truth slammed into me like you slammed into that dugong and I was a goner.'

'Yardi Creek for me,' she murmured. 'So I guess I've loved you longer.'

His smile took over his face. 'But I guarantee you I've loved you deeper.'

She curled her arms around his neck and kept him close.

'I guess we can call that a draw then. Although—' she fingered the little pearl on the chain '—I think the oyster might have known before either of us.'

He bent again for another kiss. 'Oysters always were astute.'

* * * * *

If you enjoyed this book by Nikki Logan,
look out for
STRANDED WITH HER RESCUER
also by Nikki Logan.

Or, if you'd love to read about another
gorgeous billionaire, we hope you enjoy
THE UNFORGETTABLE SPANISH TYCOON
by Christy McKellen.

Both available as eBooks!